I0831216

Hymn

Hymn

a novel

Andrew Forrest Baker

Published by Andrew F. Baker

First Edition: 2009

The characters and events in this book are fictitious. Any similarity to real persons, living or dead, is purely coincidental and not intended by the author.

All places, people, and products are notions of the author's imagination or are used fictitiously.

ISBN – 978-0-578-02951-1

cover art work by atom basham
cover design by andrew f. baker

To the writer.

To the poet.

To the gypsy.

To the vagabond.

Hymn

one

You only hear what you're wanting to hear.

The low bass of a muffler on Gaines School. The clasp of a car door closing. The rumble and whine of the engine in a truck the pizza delivery guy just got into.

You only hear what you're wanting to hear.

The soft click, click of the bicycle spokes some local artist turned into a windmill and cemented outside of the coffee shop. All the noise pollution of an early summer night in the south.

You, yourself, are hunched over a notebook on a cement patio table. You, omnipotent being that you are, know every song on every radio of every car that passes. You can hear the conversation the Sorority Girls inside are having between placing their drink orders.

"Let's have a carwash next Saturday to promote water conservation," she says. The blonde. The one wearing the hot pink Teenage Millionaire t-shirt. We are at the onset of a drought.

“I’ll have a skinny, half-caff twenty ounce latte, extra whip.” The blonde. The other one. The one with the sapphire blue eyes and matching pendant.

This is a college town, after all. The university came first. A state school. An agricultural school. Which explains the winding streets, the smell of cattle, the occasional whirlwind of white feathers on the highway. White feathers flecked in red.

This is what you’re seeing.

You only hear what you’re wanting to hear.

Doctors have labeled it a phenomenon between sexes. Between mother and child. They’ve built machines to simulate the experience. Subliminal audio advertising at the museum or Starbucks. Implants for your ears. Sound waves versus silicone. And still an inability to pinpoint a cause. The results are misleading. Notes about singular frequencies one of the professors at the University may be able to help you understand.

Omnipotent you. You know. But you’re not talking. No, tonight is for listening and listing. The pen scratch on the paper. The hippie chicks – baggy tee and ponytail; tie-died tank and dreadlocks – talking about Aderol, puppies, coffee. The CB in the cop cars. A quiet early summer night.

When you re-read this, you find yourself saying, “That’s not how it actually happened.” Auditory hallucinations. Missteps of the mind. Like song lyrics you’ve been singing wrong for years.

You tell yourself you were never that happy, sad, alone, complete. The past is rewritten by the now.

Five years ago, before the move to this agricultural hospice, before the sparks of accidental coincidence, you were another person in a different coffee shop. Old habits die hard, but you've replaced your pen several times.

It's five years earlier and you're speaking expeditiously to Mark about religion. Mark is a misnomer. So is religion.

Niels Bohr told Albert Einstein to "stop telling God what to do." Twelve-year-old Einstein who thought Euclidean geometry offered more certainty, more absolute, than god ever could. You tell Mark this.

Mark has soft black hair and Audrey Hepburn sunglasses. He's skinny, though not as skinny as you. Mark, in his white t-shirt and black cargo shorts. He looks at you in your white t-shirt and black cargo shorts. He says, "If God did not exist, it would be necessary to create Him."

Mark quotes Voltaire. Mark is a misnomer. On a birth certificate.

You have conversations like this long before you make it to University Town, Georgia. When you're supposed to be there already.

You say you want to conduct a study. You want to poll all the clergymen. The priests, the pastors, the Pope. You want the President hooked up to a polygraph machine. You want to ask them if God exists.

"Lie detectors are easy to fool."

Mark tells you this. Mark, with his oversized sunglasses and gentle sparring of chest hair. Mark the nihilist says it wouldn't work.

These are just fragments. The things you remember. Selective memory. Personalized amnesia.

These are the details you notice more. The way the espresso swirl in your latte changes. How soymilk never foams well.

Or earlier still. You at thirteen. Walking up your driveway from the school bus. Down and then up the driveway that dipped in the center. The gravel driveway with half so steep you worked up all your bicycle's momentum on the down slope just to make it back up the other side and to your house. The trailer.

You, the latchkey kid. Home from school. You at age eight.

You repeat things so you'll remember them. The details you notice more. The details the police will ask for. You repeat things like a singer, a student, an ad exec. Like lovers repeating "you," like "us." So you can remember.

Your mother ate popcorn for dinner two weeks out of each month. You thought it was a diet. You were poor and rent was due. The details the shrink would want to know. Brown shag carpet. An original Atari. Pac-man.

You with your pen are jotting down the missteps of your story. Of religion and dead chickens. University magic. Suburban Santeria.

Mark is telling you his theories on Atheism. How he was brought up Church of God. Handling snakes. Tongues taking hold of his neighbors. This was five years ago. This proves there is no god.

"God does not play dice with the universe."

You repeat things. The cold steel. The sharpness. You repeat things so you can remember.

Mark tells you that you will reinvent the Bible, if not the wheel. He says it's inside of you already, the story. You listen. You listen and list.

Mark says man created god in his image and then killed him. Man created god and then murdered him in a bloody crucifixion. In a brutal war on Mt. Olympus, in Iraq. Mark says to look at the word you just wrote. To look at crucifixion. To rewrite the last two syllables with a spell-check edit.

He says, "This explains god." Mark says this.

You only hear what you're wanting to hear.

When you move in with Mark two months later his roommate Mabel looks you up and down. She focuses briefly on your pale green eyes.

"Are you sure he's the one?" she asks.

Mark glances at your notebook.

"He's the one."

Mark tells you to meet him at St. Grace's. This is a month and a half before you move into his house. This is two weeks after you've met that first day at The Morning Bean. This is when the details are more vibrant. His stubbled jawbone chiseled sharply. The scar on the left side of his chin. Mark's scar.

You and Mark, the two of you, have continued your foray into philosophy twice a week, sipping coffee on the patio, crashing into couches.

Mark says, "Next Tuesday at three sharp. St. Grace's on McClendon. In the C Building lobby."

You show up dressed for a funeral. You feel it is appropriate to be astute in a hospital. In the terminal ward. You park your car with a sudden, embarrassing sense of irony.

This is what you're feeling.

Mark is waiting beside the sliding glass doors, his left hand nonchalantly brushing the palm frond just inside the lobby. His right hand jutting out occasionally to activate the motion sensor on the door.

He sees you and nods.

The receptionist is all smiles as you sign in. She beams a sort of compassionate understanding. She seems almost happy that above her, behind her, people are bed-ridden. People are dying. It gives her meaning.

Mark tells her your grandmother is in the cancer ward. Smoked her whole life. Terrible way to go.

The receptionist pours on the compassion: "Ms. Lackey?"

You nod along and peer to the right.

You are upstairs. The hallway is a dingy white. Fluorescent lights flicker overhead. Stainless steel carts are strewn haphazardly throughout the hallway. Orderlies are in the cafeteria. Are in the break room. Are fucking in the broom closet. Half eaten plates of off-brand gelatin stacked up on abandoned carts.

No employee wants to see the family during visiting hours. To have to smile and look at tears and pleading eyes. Not at the start of visiting hours. That's when the families of the most sick arrive. That's what Mark says.

Mark says, "You pick the first door."

Details. The ones you remember.

"Are you sure he's the one?"

Mabel is wearing a powdered wig. White dust is littering the shoulders of her grey petticoat. Black leggings. Revolutionary War Mabel. Barbie's great, great-aunt.

Mabel huffs and grabs the duffle bag from your hands. She twists a silver deadbolt in the hallway and pushes open a door, tossing your bag inside.

When she turns her back to you, you take the time to study the intricate weaving of her headpiece, to admire the simplicity of its design. The basic curls at the nape of the neck. The close-to-the-scalp wave of what you're sure is actual horsehair and the simple black ribbon that indicate the design as male.

As if she can feel your eyes on her, Mabel turns slowly to face you and smiles. She smiles crookedly, more of a sneer. The muscles in the left side of her face tensing; four teeth visible. Slightly yellowed canines. Details. She sneers and disappears down the hallway.

Your room is how Carl Jung describes death. White walls, white ceiling, white floor. A single fluorescent bulb in the center of the room glares off the blinds, sealed shut. Tight. When the door is closed you can barely make out the seam. No trim. Swinging door. No knob. A solid white cube.

"Welcome home," Mark says.

"Quaint."

You say this. Part of Jung's personality test. This is how you see death. Well, maybe not at this moment.

three

"We dope them up so they're not afraid of dying."

"I thought we did it for the pain," you say. Omnipotent you. You know the morphine drip is barely dulling. More of a sleep aid than anything. Cold comfort pumped right into the arm.

You hear the low beep of the heart monitors echo down the hallway, off the steel carts of St. Grace's Terminal Ward. You hear the swish swish, swish swish of the respirators. The dripping of a colostomy bag filling.

Two orderlies grunt and fight to turn Ms. Lackey onto her side. To avoid bedsores. Not only is Ms. Lackey dying of a tumor in her right lung, she has also managed to clog up her arteries with a lifetime of pork-n-beans and soap operas.

"Everyone on this floor is afraid of death." Mark says this. "Everyone in this hospital, in this city. These sad fucks are just closer to it than the rest of us. They've blown their load and now they're just jerking off with their asses hanging out of a white paper gown."

Mark's hand closes around the legs of the old man on the bed. Varicose veins glow a purple blue next to the man's sallow complexion. Next to

Mark's white fingers. The clipboard at the foot of the bed says: Fitzgerald, Leslie.

Mark's knuckles go whiter around Leslie's calf. Leslie mumbles in his sleep, his leg trembling slightly, too weak for any actual movement.

No one has come to visit Leslie. No one but yourself and Mark.

You think: *In the beginning, God created the onslaught of death.*

Mark says, "You're not quite there yet," grabs your hand, and leads you into the hallway.

Ten rooms later visiting hours are ending. You pass the receptionist who gives you her half smile and asks about your grandmother.

"She seems fatter," Mark says.

As if this were a compliment on the service of the hospital, the receptionist smiles again and waves you goodbye.

four

Tuesdays and Thursdays you sit out on the back porch of Mark's house. More of a stoop really. Cinderblocks and a few folding chairs. Old beer bottles for ashtrays. Sundays you work the brunch rush at The Morning Bean. Wednesdays you work the late night shift. Fridays and Saturdays you're there too. Mondays you write.

It's Thursday. You sit with a Lucky Strike half perched on your dry lips. Wafts of smoke are almost blinding and seem to dance in the passing lights of cars on the nearby Interstate. You can feel the crisscross of the woven plastic chair imprinting your ass like a chessboard. Cicadas sing between the zoom of tractor-trailers.

Mark and Mabel are to either side of you. Bodyguards against the summer heat. Mabel has forsaken her traditional garb for a black sports bra and Lycra biking shorts. Not that Mabel owns a bike. But Mabel is hot. And Mabel knows this.

Mabel, she lifts her beer to her lips and swigs long and deep. She says, "What kind of reversal of the skyline do you think it would take for people around here to stop and listen? How do you think New York is handling the deafening silence after the terrible din?"

Mabel doesn't expect an answer. Mabel poses her rhetoricals for personal, internal dissection. Mabel feels her job is to make those around her think.

Mark doesn't think. Mark answers. This is his role.

Mabel the riddler. Mark the elucidator. You.

On a lucky Tuesday night you'll see sparks. A light blue SUV will fishtail to the right and a yellow GTO will smash headfirst into the rear passenger side bumper. Headlights will slow. Cars going northbound will rubberneck into whiplash, nearly amplifying the damage. Carnage meets human engineering.

Headlights and taillights. A makeshift Christmas tree on the 85.

"Do you think they were afraid of dying? At that moment?"

"Do you think they care now?"

"Tomorrow we'll go see Leonard."

Leonard is Mark's father. You meet him first after your trip to St. Grace's. You meet him in your Sunday Best and he says, "You look like shit." Leonard with his potbelly and receding hairline. Leonard tells you you look like conformity run over.

Leonard works at the QuickSave off of Braselton Highway. He is a retired cop from Jackson County. He keeps a loaded rifle under the counter. Leonard worked death row detail, walking prisoners to their ends, recording their last words, pulling dummy levers. Pulling live levers.

"Don't believe what you read in the newspapers," Leonard says. "They're just kicking up bullshit to make the moms at home feel better about sending their kids off to Sunday School. They tell you that these men about to get burnt so bad from the inside out – about to get burnt so bad their eyeballs drip out of their head – they tell you those bastards all repent. That they found God and asked His blessing on them. That they sought redemption for their sins. That their tattooed knuckles buckled up around the arm of the chair and they smiled and welcomed Heaven.

"That's bullshit!" Leonard says. "You got ID?" he asks. "Twelve fifty."

Leonard barely glances at the identification card of the woman purchasing a pack of Virginia Slims Ultra Menthols. Leonard barely glances at the ID and he doesn't stop talking.

"Those men, they were scared shitless. Those men, they wept like little girls who found their daddy's masturbating in the corner of their bedrooms. They says, 'I'm gonna be worm food.'"

Mark counts the tubes of Monistat 7, the cartons of condoms, while Leonard talks at you from behind the counter. Mark thinks you're learning something. He expects you to take notes.

Leonard says there were thirteen executions in the state between 1983 and 1988. Leonard says he worked twelve of them. Leonard's got stories he could tell you. Secrets. Secrets that don't involve bodily fluids so much as soul-like knowledge.

Leonard says, "These men. They was white men, some of them, but mostly black. Young and old. And it didn't matter. They all knew the same goddamn thing."

Leonard says, "Smoke break."

Mark says, "Let's go."

Leonard says, "Come back by and I'll tell you about James."

Mark throws the car into reverse and is on the highway before you can buckle your seatbelt. Mark in his Audrey Hepburn sunglasses.

Mark with his gentle sparring of chest hair.

Mark says, "You don't look like shit."

five

The Morning Bean is a haven. People come here to try to discover more about themselves in cups of ground coffee beans and milk. They look for insights to appear in journal pages, on the pages of their Bible. In textbooks.

You. Omnipotent you. You grind espresso and steam milk. You wipe down counters and control the music. Tonight it's folk. You stare out the window to the elevated patio – The Morning Bean is in the basement – and watch Mark and Mabel stare back inside at you.

Omnipotent you, you hear:

"Has he written anything yet?"

"I don't think it's time."

"He should be writing by now."

"Perhaps."

You load demitasse cups and saucers into the sanitizer. You brew another pot of coffee.

"So, do you think it's going to be you or me?"

"Me. Definitely me."

Mark says this. Mark smiles slyly at Mabel. Mabel in her sports bra and cargo shorts. Mabel with her fifteen eyelet boots. Mabel with her hair pulled back and eyeliner.

Mabel says, "Shit. I should have stayed in my wigs and petticoats."

Inside the café, you hear the low whine of acoustic guitars. You shuffle the radio to NPR. You hear the low nasal voice of a news announcer. The scratch of a highlighter in a physics textbook.

This is how you spend your days. Staring at the notebook on the booth table where the make station gives way to the seating area. Wondering what holy text Mark expects you to be writing.

Six

Mark calls him Harry. Mark tells you not to stare at the red dot. Not because Harry is sensitive, but because it is disrespectful. Mark says not to stare because symbolism, despite its inconsequence, holds a kind of temporary power. A banal brainwashing. A mind-fuck.

"Nice to meet you, Harry."

"Haripreet," he corrects you.

You pull your eyes away from the circular sparkle on his forehead and force your eyes around the apartment. An Urban Outfitter's look at modern chic, with aged-gold statues of Indian gods nestled on bookshelves, above the television. Except these statues are not resin knockoffs or plastic replicas. They are older, hand-painted and efficiently delicate. They rest on alters of intent.

"Mark tells me you're interested in converting to Hindu."

Haripret speaks his words slowly, with the kind of patience he would tell you only the gods had the power to grant. With the gentle word choice of sincerity that comes from belief. Harry says "Haripreet" means "beloved of gods" so you've come to the right place.

The pompousness that comes with religion.

"I thought only women wore the red dot," you say in response.

"*Tilaka*. Men wear them during ceremony. It symbolizes the third-eye. I am in the midst of a forty day fast."

The smell of incense is overwhelming. *Dhoop*. Cloves and cardamom. You notice the oil lamps on each table. The straw yoga mat rolled up in the corner.

"Wait a second," you say. "Forty days without food?"

"It's a simple austerity, really," Haripreet exudes, his eyes downcast. Diminutive pride. "Please be seated."

Haripreet drops slowly to the floor, crossing his legs in the half-lotus position. Mark's hand grasps your shoulder and squeezes. He opens the door and is gone before you can join Haripreet on the floor.

seven

Haripreet is silent for a moment. Finding balance. Calming his inner eye. Tuning out the auditory advertisements of a nuclear age in the southern U.S.

You sit in antsy reverence, trying to look serene. You glance toward the doorway without twisting your head so as not to appear uninterested or disrespectful. You wonder where the hell Mark decided he needed to be and how the hell you are going to get home if he has gone. You cleanse your inner eye and stop yourself from scratching at your forehead.

When Haripreet looks into your eyes he is calm. He is smiling. His brown skin shows very few of the lines that rise up from worry. His smile lines are deep.

"There is much debate amongst the Indian community regarding one's rights and abilities to convert to Hinduism," he says. You should be taking notes. "Most believe that Hindu is something one is born into. Caste systems are in place. Reincarnation is reliant among the caste system. This is central to our beliefs.

"My guru in India taught me much. He believes as I do. We believe that one who seeks out our gods may be shown the way of light."

As he speaks, Haripreet's olive skin sparkles with the sustained animation of a Saturday morning cartoon character, of a late night TV talk show host, of a later night Television evangelist. His black hair is rich and milky, almost green where the light hits it, and cropped short, dolloped into place with pomade.

"I can not promise a conversion that would be recognized in the Temples of my homeland."

Haripreet looks at you as if this is a question. Like he is a textbook. Spurting knowledge, expounding truths. As if he needs a "yes, sir, master, sir" in order to proceed. You stare back trying to imbue a state of serenity. All doe-eyed and bushy-tailed.

He smiles broader and closes his eyes, as if he is waiting on you to meditate on your answer. The *dhoop* is getting to you. You find your voice.

"So what would conversion entail? Perhaps if I know more, I can understand if this is the proper path."

You pride yourself on your textbook answer.

"I can only begin you on your journey," Haripreet intones. "And be warned that this is a long journey. It would begin with a *shuddhikaran* ritual and culminate in your rebirth."

Although these words seem ominous, Haripreet speaks them with revelry, as if he is beginning to see himself transcend. Haripreet the guru.

Haripreet explains that a *shuddhikaran* is a cleansing ritual. Your head will be shaved. Your body will be washed. A baptism. An anointment. An easier way to clean your diaper.

Haripreet tells you that this life is only the first step. He says your soul will be reborn into Hindu and your conversion will thus be complete. Haripreet says this.

"When I light incense it carries my desires with it to the gods."

Haripreet says, "How do you feel about death?"

eight

"Would we be able to survive a world without gods? If not a symbolic 'power,' then items, celebrities— money. We glom onto concepts and material goods like incense to your hair."

"Maybe that's why they shave your head for the cleansing ritual."

Mabel thinks she's being cute. Mabel in her powder grey petticoat. Mabel with flakes from her powdered white wig sifting with the breeze to land on her shoulders. You wondering how she does it as you're sweating in your white tank top. You stare at Mark for an answer. Mark in his Hunter Green shorts and Emergency Orange flip-flops.

"Think of these as a series of vignettes," she says.

Mabel dumps a bag of small videocassettes onto the twin-sized iron framed mattress in the corner of your bedroom. Tank Girl Mabel in her knee high combat boots. You stare at her from the high backed desk chair across the room. Mabel with her accessory bag of videocassettes.

"These are from when I first met Mark. I figured it could help you out with your project."

"What am I supposed to be doing?"

You say this in all seriousness. You, omnipotent you, concerned that you are failing at some job. Some position you were hired to fulfill.

"You're a writer. Write."

"And what are these?"

"I used to be a filmmaker," Mabel says. She sighs and stacks the videocassettes into neater piles. Eighteen. Three stacks of six.

Mabel with her long black hair not hidden under a wig. Mabel with black too-short shorts. Her too tight tank top. Mabel sighs and looks at you.

"Pray it's not you."

If you look confused, it's because you are.

"Pray to whom?"

Mabel considers this for a moment. She glances through the numbered videotapes, biting her bottom lip. Tape 6. Tape 11. Tape 2.

Finally she looks up.

"Mark."

Insert Mark and Mabel's history. Their background. Mabel met Mark at sixteen, when she was still in high school. Mabel with her too-short pixie cut. Fishnet and amulets. Mabel is Siouxie Sioux before her hips were fully rounded.

Mabel is in Sculpture class. Outside in the courtyard working with her hands. Mabel shifts at random intervals so she doesn't get any clay onto her flowing black skirt. Mabel keeps glancing at Mark.

Mark in the courtyard. Mark skipping class. On campus. Mark propped up on a bench reading Nietzsche.

"Your bust is crooked."

Mabel wipes her hands on the grass and begins adjusting her corset, playing with the laces. Mabel, worried about the A-cup she's been working on.

"Yeah, well.... Your book is upside down."

You don't know if this is true. This is how Mabel tells the story.

Mark. He laughs. Rare and infectious. The left side of Mark's face tightens, eye squinting, lips drawing up in a smirk. A sneer. Mark stands and crosses the yard to Mabel.

"I was talking about the statue."

Mabel stops fiddling with her clothing and takes in her work. Still headless, she can see Satan emerging from the greedy loins of two nymphs spiraled on a pedestal. Still headless. Not technically a bust. Mabel notices the pitchfork is angled improperly. She adjusts her bell sleeves.

"Fuck the statue," Mabel says, punching in the opposite side in an act of defiance. To even it out a little. "I'm just doing this for class. I'm a filmmaker."

Mark's smile returns. More of a sneer every time. More so every time so that now, Mabel says, now he has lost the ability to give a simple smile.

"Do you want to make a movie?"

This is three months before Mark starts fucking Mabel, Mabel tells you. She says:

"So that gives you about two weeks."

Mabel says, "You might want to hide these." She scatters the videocassettes across the mattress and stacks them up neatly once more. "Not under the bed."

Mabel stands in the center of your room. The fluorescent a spotlight on her head. Her skin almost merging with the walls. Her black hair and black clothes in stark contrast with the room. Porcelain Doll Mabel.

Mabel says to pray it's not you. Pray unto Mark, she says.

"Get out while you can."

ten

You're thinking, *get a fucking clue, bitch.* You're thinking, *how the hell did you slip through the penal code*? You're thinking, *Mark was right.* Mark tells you you'll have to keep an open mind with this one. Mark tells you this. Mark the nihilist atheist. Mark is right.

You. You're standing in the porch-turned-sunroom of Ambyrr Lytte-Prism. Twelve cats prance in figure eights around your feet. Two more muddled calicos sit primly on the floral print cushion of the wicker couch. You try to inhale the scent of the lavender and rosemary growing in the corner. You try to breathe in the thyme and anise. You try to find any plant growing in the room that can mask the near medicinal scent of cat piss. Of the cat piss of 14 cats. Getting stronger.

"They like you," Ambyrr says. "Well, except for Zeus and Hera."

Ambyrr motions to the king and queen calico residing from their wicker throne. Hera, or maybe Zeus, squeezes her eyelids shut and stares back at you.

"Don't feel bad though." Ambyrr says this to comfort you. "They can just sense that you have power. A strong power. They get the same way around Mark. He's got it too."

Mark. Mark who dropped you off at 10:15 this morning. Mark who didn't even get out of the car to offer up an introduction. Mark who had warned you to keep an open mind.

Ambyrr is still talking:

"Mister Fuzzy-Wuzzy here gets all jealous when there are other powerful males around. Doesn't he? Doesn't he?" The only way you can tell Ambyrr's baby-talk is directed toward the cat she's petting and not you is the slightly higher pitch in her voice. "It's not enough for him to be a rare male calico. No, he's got to be the man of the house too."

Suddenly, Ambyrr remembers you.

"Is that why you're here?"

Your eyes reflexively go wide with fear as you imagine Ambyrr inviting you to become the man of her house. You begin to stammer before she speaks again.

"To learn to develop your power? Because I can show you some things, but I'm just not too sure I could really help you fully develop. I mean, I can do a spell or two. I am very close with the god and goddess. I understand the logistics of things, but —quite honestly— I do not possess the natural energies inherent in most magical peoples. But I have heart and that's really all that...."

"No," you try to get a word in edgewise. "I... well; Mark was hoping I could just sit with you for a while. Discuss the intricacies of your world. Find out what exactly it takes to run a neo-pagan website."

"Oh! Mark isn't trying to get in on the neo-pagan site world, is he?" Ambyrr laughs. She laughs as if this is funny. "I don't need the competition." More laughter.

You glance across the room to the laptop perched open on the tiny polished oak desk. You notice three Starbucks cups on the desk. You notice a trashcan overflowing with more beside the desk chair.

I could use some coffee, you think. You think *it's going to be a very long day*.

"Oh, what fun!" Ambyrr squeals.

Everything in the room is fighting for your attention. Researchers could have a hay day with this. All this multi-consciousness advertising. Scent, sight, and sound. Except instead of rewarding you with a hamburger, you're left with urine and a slight buzz in your ear. Whiz and onomatopoeia.

In an effort to tune her out, you take note of Ambyrr's demeanor. She stands up as straight as she can. Probably insecure about her slight, five-foot two-inch frame. She jostles back and forth in her platform shoes as if she must keep moving to find balance. Like a bicyclist on a tightrope. Her hands flail as she speaks, going to her frizzy brown hair as she pauses for breath, soothing it back behind the red and brown head wrap she no doubt picked up at the last Wiccan retreat to some secluded state campgrounds.

The rest of her, clad in a white tank top and tie-dyed sari, is pale and freckled. Her fingernails are cut short and show no signs of ever having seen polish. She smiles her words from behind thin red lips. A bubblegum machine pentacle hangs from a brown leather strap at her clavicle.

"I like your tattoos," you say, eyeing her left bicep. The Triple Goddess Moon banded with Celtic knot work.

Ambyrr smiles and holds her arm out like a chicken wing to admire her own work. She twists to show you her right arm. This one a series of blue and purple butterflies touching the tips of their wings to one another in a sort of insect maypole dance.

The whole time she is talking. Chatting. Gossiping. She is telling you where and when each tattoo came about. She is describing each line of ink in detail. She is asking you a question.

"No, not yet," you offer. "I haven't really found a design I'm comfortable with."

"Oh!" Ambyrr exclaims. "Go to the mall. They have this awesome store there. All sorts of stickers and postcards and journals and stuff. I got this one from one of the stickers they had there! I mean, there were so many, it was hard to choose...."

Ambyrr is lifting the front of her tank top. Ambyrr is showing you a fairy with a fucked-up face perched atop a red and green mushroom. Red mushroom with green spots. And the fairy in black and white striped tights.

You find yourself wishing a house would drop out of the sky.

On Ambyrr, not the fairy. The fairy's fine.

eleven

Flashes of red. Sparks of light glancing off of silver. More red. Massive amounts of red. And you. This is four years ago. Four years before now. This is one year after you meet Mark. This is ten months after Mabel leaves. After Mabel leaves you her videocassettes. These are the details you remember.

Mark and his meetings for you. Mark and his cavalcade of characters for you to interview, to write about. Mark and his dinner parties. Mark and his sex.

Aristotle says that "Memory is neither Perception nor Conception, but a state or affection of one of these, conditioned by lapse of time." Aristotle says this in 350 B.C.E. Before Jesus Christ. Aristotle says this and you remember it now. Jesus remembers it too.

The lapses in time that muddle things. These are the flashes of red. The glint of a knife. The details the police will want to know.

A therapist can put you under a marginal hypnosis to recall the subtexts you have forgotten. There are clues. Hints. Triggers.

Scents and colors and words and shapes. Things that will push you over the rainbow. Technicolor brilliance. Dancing midgets.

Mark says, "Write it all down. You can edit it later."

Mark says, "Write it all down."

So you can remember.

And there you are, saying *that's not how it happened.* Saying you *were never that happy or alone. Sad or complete.*

"Looks like it's just us boys," Mark says. "You want to go out later? What do you want for dinner?"

Mark is standing in your doorway, leaning really, against the frame, and smiling at you sitting with your notebook. His grey eyes glance around the room and are met with white walls. White blinds, sealed tight.

Mark says, "We don't necessarily have to go out, though." He is smiling broadly as he says this.

"Where's Mabel?" you ask. "Why's it 'just us boys' tonight?" Not that you're concerned. Not that you really care.

"Mabel moved out. While you were at work last night."

Mark tells you this still smiling. Smirking. Sneering. Mark's smile. He tells you this as if it's no big deal. That this person he's known for five years – that he fucked for two of those – packed up her shit and hit the road.

Mark's inside your room now. He's peeking through the blinds. White light pours in. Carl Jung's Death. Mark's finger traces a path across the wall. Sweat and bodily fluids to warp the paint for a different generation to discover. Mark's own cave paintings. Hieroglyphs.

Mark says, "I'm thinking barbeque."

You're thinking *Fried Green Tomatoes.*

Mark says, "So Mabel didn't tell you goodbye? She said she was going to. She decided to move back to her parent's house for a while. To save some money for college. They live about two hours south of here. She's going to try to come back up for the Fourth."

Of July. You tell Mark Mabel must have forgotten. Adios. Oh well. Take care. Forget to write.

"Hey," Mark says. Mark says as if it just crossed his mind. "Did Mabel leave anything in here for you? She said she had a gift or you."

You tell Mark she must have forgotten that as well.

"Eh. Maybe she'll remember when she's back up next month."

Mark sits on the edge of your bed, forcing you to turn in your desk chair to see his face. Mark's face. With the smile lines on the left deeper than the right. Mark's face, with the black stubble that peeks through even after he's straight razored. Mark's face, contorting.

"Damn," he says. Mark says this as if it's just crossed his mind. "How can you sleep on this thing? Maybe we should turn the mattress."

You remind Mark that you've only been here for two months. Two months today. You say, "Isn't that a once a year thing?" and Mark, Mark is already pulling off the sheets to pile on top of the pillow he tossed to the floor.

"You get the top end."

That's not how it really happened. These are just details altered by time. Perceptions. Diagnosed with amnesia. The things you chose to remember.

Mark and his crooked sneer, sitting on the freshly turned bed, still devoid of sheets, of comfort, saying "Now doesn't this feel better?"

You, omnipotent you completely unaware of what the hell is going on. You sitting next to him.

Him saying, "No, you've got to get closer to the center. Where you sleep. That's where you'll feel it."

And then Mark's hands. Mark's lips. Still sneering. Pressed against yours. Mark's t-shirt tangled up on the floor. Your pants.

Mabel's words flash into your head. The taste of stale smoke. Cigarettes and coffee. Work. The Morning Bean. Mark. Mabel.

"Get out while you can."

thirteen

They keep them behind a soundproof glass. Behind glass and in a sea of isolated bins. Near the back, the bins are enclosed, dripping fluid and pumping oxygen. They keep them away from where they came into being. So they won't hear the screaming. The pain. So their mothers can rest.

Mark is hinting at dichotomy. He has you, the proud father-to-be, standing and tapping at the glass of the nursery at St. Grace's. Listening to the dads and grandparents giggling and pointing at the little baby boy in the pale blue blanket. At the red and splotchy baby in the pink.

"Which one is yours?" two joyous lips beneath a puffed white wig ask from your left.

Mark has seen the little one she and her family have been goo-ing and gaa-ing to. He points to a little boy a few bins over. His skin is a pitch black and he has not stopped crying since you arrived. Not that you can hear through the soundproof glass, but he looks miserable.

"That little gem is ours," Mark beams. His arm wraps around your waist and he presses a smirk against your cheek. "We're so ecstatic!"

The white wig smiles and retreats a few steps. "That poor boy," she whispers to the liver spots on her husband's cheekbone.

You totally fucking agree, Lady.

Mark says, "The miracle of life is only miraculous when it's your own."

Mark clasps your hand and leads you down to the delivery ward. You slip past orderlies and into a pair of blue paper scrubs that look incredibly awkward wrapped around you. Your jeans and combat boots peeking out. Mark in cargo shorts clearly visible from the poorly tied backing of the suit. You fit right in with the other terrified and nervous fathers dancing through the ward hallways.

People are so tied up in their own worlds — the seeming awakenings, the utter miracles going on around them that nearly everyone who passes fails to notice the two of you. Constantly in the hallway. Never entering a room. Teetering around from doorway to doorway looking to hear anything scream or cry or beg to be shot in the face.

This is another lesson for you. This is the time in between when Mark returns as your teacher, your mentor. These are the notes he expects you to be taking. To be twisting into prose – an epic poem as long as the Odyssey. Disproving the fiction of epics past. These are the words he wants you to write. Mark tells you the story is already inside of you. Begging to be told. He says you just need to find the wording; the inspiration. That he can't write this because it's your story to tell.

"Not to be all Biblical on you or anything."

Mark is listening to the panicked screams of a natural-birth mother in the final throws of contractions. She is begging for a morphine drip. Urging the doctors to rip that thing out of her. That thing. Her miracle.

You are sure there is another sneering smirk behind Mark's surgical mask. You can see the lines around his left eye are tight in amusement. His eyes are sparkling from the experience.

He grabs your hand and leads you down the hallway toward the exit, ripping off his blue paper robe and letting it crumple to the tile floor.

You tell Mark you cannot go to The Morning Bean when he's forced you to call in sick for your Wednesday night late shift. You tell him you don't feel at all comfortable with this.

And where do you end up?

If you thought it would be somewhere else, you were wrong — semi-delusional. And Mark is telling Jessica that you really are a lot sicker than you look. And that it could help you feel better if you were in surroundings you were used to. Doctor's orders. Jessica who has already worked four hours and has agreed to tack on another five more with a "Get Well" wish. Jessica who is so sweet she offered to bring you soup when the shift ended. Your shift. The one she's covering. Jessica who's so naïve she is eating up every word Mark throws at her. Jessica who is so horny from lack of a serious fucking in nine and three quarter months — she's tracking — she would believe anything Mark's grey eyes batted her way.

Jessica waves to you on the patio and puts on a chamomile mint tea to help clear your lungs. To help your breathing.

Mark winks at you through the window, pays Jessica with a five from the tip jar, and is walking out to join you as Jessica turns to load the sanitizer with saucers. Mark places the tea next to your pack of cigarettes and draws one out, lighting it and inhaling deeply before sitting in the plastic seat across from your own. You reach for the pack and Mark tsks you.

"You're sick, remember."

How could you forget?

Mark is smiling in at Jessica, making a spectacle of blowing his cigarette smoke away from you. Sweet, caring Mark. Always so concerned.

Mark. He says, "The concept behind reproduction proves utterly and wholly that there is no god, despite what religion you adhere to. What kind of god would create a species designed to start over every thirty years or so? To never progress their learning beyond a genial workforce striving for an unachievable 'more?'"

These are Mark's ideas. This is the story you'll tell.

"I mean, we definitely have breakthroughs from century to century. But in the end it's all a giant game of Nintendo. And we keep hitting the goddamned reset button – shooting out infants like it's some sort of mystery how a cock and a cunt could create a whining missed abortion – and hoping the blotchy red thing will know the right key combination to ascend. Or at least skip to level eight. Right right left A B."

Video game rhetoric for the technologically impaired.

"In the end our species is Animal. Guttural. Unintelligent. Screaming non sequiturs to make our instincts known."

Flash to the Discovery Channel.

"We eat and fuck and shit and everything we say has been said by someone else in a much more intelligent way. We try to simplify and then have to work a sixty-hour workweek to afford the simplicity. An instant coffee machine ends up costing you five hours of your life at minimum wage."

Mark really hates children.

"I really hate kids."

fourteen

You only see what you're wanting to see.

This, Mark says, is the mantra for every religious person of the world. If you believe hard enough, you can see a miracle. A thunderclap of relief. A sigh of wellness washing over a cancer ward. If you believe strong enough, you will see god's face. All bumpy and translucent in the clouds. If you don't believe... Well, that's just because you don't want to see the proof around you.

You only see what you're wanting to see.

Tonight, what you're seeing is nothing near what you were hoping to see. Although it is totally what you were expecting. The fluorescent gaze of track lighting is pushing you along, sleepwalking through the MegaMart aisles of generic clothing and vitamins, condoms and week old fruit. Your fellow shoppers —the people who dwell in University Town, Georgia with you— tonight they are your zombies, grunting and groaning and reaching for sunglasses at 2am.

This is your typical night of the now. Five years later and post your nightly coffee shop endeavors into notebooks. This is you shopping for a new spiral bound, maybe a new pack of Pilot pens.

You try not to stare at the people passing by you. Leaning against shopping carts. Children passed out in the seats, with boxes of Fruity Chocolaty Sugary Cereal thrown haphazardly behind them. These people. They are dressed in oversized sweat pants with moth-chewed holes at the ankles. The elastic so stretched and pulled it must gather all its force to simply hold the pants over the bulk of a stomach gone to too little learning and too many Juju Beans. These are the sallow cheeks of a life of lower education in a college town. This is the fluorescent lighting.

The fraternity brothers whose hair has that constant curl around their Go Team hats. They are laughing and drunk and avoiding roadblocks. They are too ashamed to go back to their dorm rooms and only have their right hand to fuck. Their left one too, if it's a good night.

Even without your omnipotence, you would know their stories. You and everyone else have encountered these people in thousands of supermarkets in hundreds of towns on any given weeknight.

You stroll along casually through the produce section. You pass the day-old bakery. You spell your name on a white frosted cake in blue and pink squeeze icing. You try to appear intent and fascinated. Not that the employees at this hour care. Not that they would at any hour.

When you reach the lunch meats, your eyes dart to the kosher section. Beef two slots away from the milk.

And now you're seeing black curly hair. Short for a woman's. Piled on top of a petite frame and a large nose. Some people can't resist the stereotype. Even if they say they are above it.

This is Clara Goldstein. Clara with the mop of black curls and the wire framed glasses. Clara who married a rabbi fifteen years ago. Clara, whose ten-year anniversary was the day before Mark dropped you off at her office. Clara Goldstein, DDS PC.

fifteen

Clara Goldstein smiles at you from behind a large oak desk. It's one of those prim smiles you see planted precisely on the bulldog mug of the bitchy school marm when way-a-day parents drop their little girls off at boarding school in those old black-and-white movies. Her smile says:

I'll take good care of you.

No need to worry.

Hell has just been a figment of your imagination.

Everything on Clara's desk that isn't a stark white printout clad in manila is that shiny gold-brass you see in the corporate office suite sets at Office Depot. You fight an urge to fidget with the knife-styled letter opener as Clara gives you the up-and-down her profession requires. Her hands stay firmly grasped in front of her, harlot red polish on her nails.

Already she can tell: You don't have insurance. Your last physical was in seventh grade. Your teeth have not been cleaned since high school.

And she can read your mind. As if on cue, her smile broadens. Two perfect rows of white picket teeth blind you, forcing your gaze up to her glass-shielded eyes. She squints slightly, telling you she sees her wire frames as her only flaw. But she wears them well.

"Mark says you've been his dentist since he was eight."

You figure it's up to you to break the silence with menial small talk. If nothing else just to get the ball rolling.

Clara continues to smile.

"How long have you been in practice?"

"As a Jew?"

"As a dentist."

"Right, but that's not why you're really here." All of Clara's statements cut into yours before you can complete your final syllable. Clara, the efficient dentist. "Mark tells me you're writing a paper on Judaism for your humanities class in school. We can simply cut to the chase. Shouldn't you be taking notes?"

You almost expect Clara to burst into song at this point. Her words are scripted and musical. You can hear the fiddler tuning up.

To farputst *is to doll up... The* goyim *are all....*

"Well, where do you want to begin?" The ball is so obviously in Clara's court.

Clara sits quietly, eyes locked on you as you fumble around for a notebook and pen. Her hands firmly on her desk, you can almost see her legs crossed at the ankles behind the oak mammoth between the two of you. She smiles as you poise your pen and look forward expectantly.

"Muhammad called us the 'People of the Book,' so why don't we begin with the *Tanakh*? I'm sure you're already familiar with the five books of the *Torah*. You are Christian, correct?"

"Um. I'm not really all that sure at this point."

"Oh, don't tell me you're toying with agnosticism! Do you really have to be so dreadfully 'college'?"

Clara's smile broadens as you double take from your notebook. Could she actually be making a joke? Even still, she cuts her smile short:

"The *Torah* consists of the first five books of the Old Testament. Along with the *Nebi'im* and the *Ketuvim*, these are the sacred texts of Judaism. *Tanakh* is actually a acronym if that'll help you remember for your essay."

You give a closed-lip smile to Clara as she explains the basis of Jewish Law. The idea of the textual *mitzvot* to explain the day-to-day usage of these wisdoms, as opposed to the church-by-church rantings of some pastor or priest you were raised knowing, fascinates you. The image of Orthodox kids lining up to learn Hebrew is amusing.

Clara tells you how she was raised Reform and upon marrying Emanuel she converted to Orthodox.

"Manny and I celebrated ten years together yesterday," she smiles. The first truly genuine smile you've seen thus far. Then, as if catching herself in her revelry, Clara intones, "The thing to keep in mind about Judaism as a whole is that it's a way of life — an adherence to a moral code — more so than an observance of God. Some extremely liberal Jews don't even believe in God."

"So, being married to a rabbi, do you believe in God?"

"Well, isn't *that* the question?"

Sixteen

You take the bus home from Dr. Goldstein's office, crammed beside a well-dressed black woman with more bags than shoulders, expounding a religious sermon to no one in particular. As if that's what you needed more of right now. The man in front of you crumples his paper every few minutes in an attempt to hide the gas he's spewing out. The kids behind you think spitballs are funny.

Whoever says public transportation is the great equalizer obviously has never had to take the 113 down Northside Drive.

Mark watches you make the half-block trek down the street. He's smiling as he lights a cigarette from the front stoop, exhaling long and hard before he ventures any sound.

"The VCR's broken. I fucked it up somehow," he greets you. "Too much rewind, fast forward, and pause, I guess. Drop in your bag and we'll head up to bum dinner off my parents. It's always nicer to ask for money when you actually pay them a visit. Or we could just shuck the VCR and stick with the DVD player."

You think of Mabel's videocassettes.

"No, no. Let's go on up. Free food, right?"

"I somehow knew you'd say that."

It's what you'd expect from a made for TV movie. Not one of those Lifetime deals. No battered women or miscarriages. Just a sort of Old Yeller mystique. Vast fields lined with a few groves of evergreens and oaks. A couple of stables. A methane smell mixed with cinnamon from a fresh piecrust. Betty Ann Crocker in the kitchen with a blue dress and red plaid apron. Well, minus the Crocker part. But her name really is Betty Ann.

When your car pulls up the gravel driveway, you can see her wipe her hands on a dishtowel and step out onto the porch to join Leonard. Her sixties housewife bouffant, salt-n-pepper style, holds in stark contrast to Leonard's gruff physique. Together they make up Mark. You can see it so clearly. The guttural and grotesque and the strangely irresistible.

"Hi, boys. Mark, you want to come help me out in the stables for a minute? I got a mare hollering up to high Heaven."

Betty Ann sniffs the air.

"Oh, my! I've got an apple pie burning in the oven. Come on in, dear. Let's get you up out of this heat. How 'bout a nice glass of milk, and I'll get you a slice of pie when it cools."

Betty Ann's kitchen is covered in cattle. Ceramic cows wearing tutus. Porcelain chaps and cowboy hats on spotted dairy cows. Fairy wings on bulls. Even the wallpaper has black and white stripes, red bulls and spotted bovine, nose-to-nose, tail-to-tail. And Betty Ann is all smiles as she places the pie on the windowsill to cool. She's all ear-to-ear as she pours you a glass of milk from a thick glass carafe. She's grinning so wide her eyes are squinting slots as she turns to you, handing you the glass with the cow, and says:

"So you're the one fucking my son."

This is supposed to be linear. Everything your writing professors told you about beginnings, middles, and ends... People are supposed to receive knowledge in a certain fashion. Makes it easier to process. And even still you find yourself going all David Lynch on the narrative. This is just the way you remember things.

You remember taking a moment to stammer, to fumble with the glass bull in your hands. And Betty Ann's smile shining all of its country crock goodness like a talk show guest with Tourette's. Looking at you for an answer to her statement like she asked you what color your t-shirt is. And maybe she did. Maybe that's all she's asked at this point. And you're turning bright red for no reason.

Betty Ann looks at her watch.

"Gosh!" she says. "I guess it's too close to dinner time to be fooling around with slices of pie. You go get Mark and Leonard rounded up, and you all get yourselves scrubbed up and to the table."

You find Mark and Leonard ducked behind a clapboard stable. Marlboro Men resting on hay bales. Except they're not smoking Reds.

"You want a hit?" Leonard offers up the joint. "I know Betty Ann can be a fucking wackjob sometimes."

You take a hit and exhale slowly, falling into a coughing fit. Mark slaps your back and musses your hair.

"God's green Earth, eh?"

You pull down the driveway after an incredibly uncomfortable dinner, wondering how they had managed to pull out your entire life story over the roasted chicken and mashed potatoes. Surprised at how much Mark seemed to already know.

"Fuck!" he exclaims suddenly. "I forgot to ask for extra cash. Well, I guess we're fine with just the DVDs, huh?"

seventeen

Telephones buzzing digital bells, pushing through wires past thousands of gentrified homes. Edison plus Bell equals forced connection. Or an answering machine. Either way.

No hellos.

"Has he started writing yet?"

"A little."

"Did he watch the tapes?"

"No clue. He's kept them pretty well hidden."

"Good boy."

And sometimes silence isn't awkward.

"Should I come back early?"

eighteen

In Mark's opinion, you should be writing more.

According to Mark, the individual outweighs the mass. Yet the mass provides the hypothesis of truth. Overalls appear much easier than singulars. Moving mountains versus grains of sand. Whatever.

He says time and experience cloud things. Memories. He tells you this then. For then and now.

He offers you a new notebook. Sweet generous Mark. Every time you suck him off, another paper manufacturer gets a dollar.

So you write.

You expound on brown eyes and smile lines. How transcendence seems secular. How god is based on birth.

You discuss men dying. Dripping eyeballs Wes Craven could never really attain.

You pour out words like fourteen cats scratching at wicker furniture.

You try to remember everything you can and write it all down. You can edit it later.

And as your words slip slowly away from you, you stare into your closet at the eighteen videocassettes Mabel left behind. You stare at the fifty-three dollars and seventy-three cents tucked into the shoes you never wear anymore. All your tip money from the last week and a half. You think in two week's time you should be able to get one of those kid's room TV/VCR duos for the break room at The Morning Bean.

nineteen

Attending a Catholic Mass is a lot like going to a magic show. There's a huge focus on the showy slight-of-hand. An absurd amount of flashy colors and symbolism. You're never completely sure if the man on stage is straight. And of course there's the ultimate disappearing act.

Check out God's lovely assistant. Now move the stone and... TADAA! He's gone!

Then just as quickly a whoosh! and He's back.

Except this time He doesn't owe the magician a hummer in the dressing room. Now He's simply got the burden of a million years of sin and indulgence He never got to experience first-hand. Talk about the alpha and omega of letdowns.

Mark. He thinks this Sunday morning excursion will do you some good.

"For a trinity of reasons," he smiles.

For starters, it will help you better understand and deal with Ambyrr Lytte-Prism since, Mark says, paganism is a lot like Catholicism in it's gaudy penchant for ritual; saints as gods as saints as angels. Plus it'll prep you for your upcoming appointment with some Iyagwo you can't remember the name of. Because apparently Santeria is based entirely off of the Catholic faith. Or rather a traditional African faith glued behind the martyrs smiling from their seven-day candles.

And finally, you will be meeting Matthew Brohmer. Matthew is an avid member of the Church and, Mark says, is that guy in his mid-30s sitting in the second pew, three people over from the television cameraman.

There're another two cameramen in the balcony. And one to the left of the pulpit who's operating a big crane to swoop down over the congregation during the musical numbers so the at-home parishioners can fully understand the scope of the hymns. Like the Holy Spirit is descending upon the decadence. Your own hallowed point of view.

You know you should be focusing on God. You know this because all of a sudden He's capitalized. You know this, yet you're completely distracted by the glorious beams of colored light dancing through Peter, Paul, and Mary; glowing through the Christ Child or the Archangel Michael in stained glass. The grotesque effigy of a man way too ripped to be starving, crowned and nailed to a Roman torture device captures your gaze. You stare at ornately carved columns. You question what's been said inside that confession booth. You imagine alter boys and helping hands. You pay attention to everything except the sermon.

And then there's Mark. Mark who, surprisingly, seems totally enamored with the priest's words. Mark whose smirk stretches further and further across his face as Biblical torments are forced upon follower after follower. Mark who refuses to lower his eyes in prayer.

You and Mark are in the third to last row of pews, below the balcony overhang. They have a clause when you come in warning you that, if you are not planning to receive communion during the service, you have to sit in the balcony or in the five rear rows of the lower level. That way, the cameras catch only empty seats as they pan across the flock moving forward for some old fashioned cannibalism. Symbolic cannibalism. But those aren't their words.

As the priest's throat begins to dry out from extolling the virtues of the body of Christ, Mark pulls you to your feet and out through the wooden doors of the Gothic cathedral for a cigarette.

"Nicotine is so much more rewarding than a cracker," he says.

"But the cracker gets you closer to God."

That wasn't you.

"Matt!" Mark laughs and extends his hand.

Matthew Brohmer shakes Mark's hand and smiles in your direction. It's a smile you'd expect Jesus to boast after turning water into wine or bee-lining across the Sea of Galilee. All full of the arrogance that accompanies an I-betcha-didn't-know-I-could-do-that wink.

"Hey listen," Matt says. "There's a group of us that head over to the Sizzler for Sunday brunch every week. You want to join us? A six-point perspective could be a lot more interesting than just mine."

Of course you know Mark won't let you out of this. Of course you know he won't be accompanying you. You. All you can do is suck it up, hop into the light blue mini-van and buckle up.

twenty

With the Sunday afternoon lunch special, you can get an all-you-can-eat taste extravaganza for under seven dollars. Even adding a large sweet tea will only set you back another dollar and a half. And, if that is not enough to tempt you towards the pre-prepared steak and aluminum foil wrapped baked potatoes, the snazzy sneeze guard protecting the gummy bears, bananas, and three different kinds of generic pudding is there to ceil the deal.

You end up with a chicken breast and a scoop of macaroni and cheese, not because it's what you particularly want, but because you aren't as adept at dodging the hippos storming the watering hole. Your plate looks practically barren as you sit it down next to the five others loading your table. Matt Brohmer shushes Shelia Arbuckle from groaning out some comment about anorexia as you move to sit down.

"Oh my goddess. It is you!!"

The last thing you expect to see here is frizzy brown hair and a red and orange body wrap. But there they are, standing in stark contrast to the grey on grey carpeting and polished oak veneer tables.

"Hi, Ambyrr," you smile. "I didn't think I'd catch you eating here."

"Oh, I'm not. I'm a strict vegetarian and well— Eeek!" she nods her head toward the buffet line. "My mom's in town, and she absolutely loves this place. Old people, you know? Oh! Who are your friends?"

Ambyrr's foot seems to reside in her mouth. But she never notices. No, she just plays it off as if every word she spills out crosses her tongue before it even registers in her head. And maybe that's true.

"Oh, this is...."

"Matthew Brohmer." He stands to shake her hand. "And this is Claudette Mills. Shelia Arbuckle. Clinton Carmichael. Gayle Pitts. And Pat Carlisle."

"It's very nice to meet you guys. I'm Ambyrr Lytte-Prism. Are you guys— Where are you guys coming from all dressed up? Did somebody croak? Oh my goddess, did Mark croak? I never even saw an obituary!"

Ambyrr is looking at you like you've betrayed her suddenly.

"We're just having a nice, *quiet* meal after church."

That was Gayle. Gayle is dressed like Jackie O' in a dove grey number. Her pillbox hat is bobby pinned to grey hair frozen in place with half a can of White Rain. You smile to yourself as you wonder what would happen if she tried using that shit on her face to iron out some of her wrinkles. Pull and spray, honey. Pull and spray.

Meanwhile, Ambyrr's hurt is quickly turning to confusion. And she's not going anywhere.

"We meet here every Sunday after mass," Pat offers.

"Oh!" Ambyrr suddenly exclaims, looking completely relieved. "You're Catholics! So this is like your coven."

"Why, I never...."

Gayle again.

"Oh, you know what I mean," Ambyrr trudges on. "Congregation, coven; Mary, Mother Goddess; Potato, Potahtoe."

"Well, Ambyrr," you offer up a quick distraction from either the comments or the shocked faces —you're not too sure which— and place your hand on the insane pagan's shoulder. "I bet your mom's waiting on you."

If you didn't know better, you'd swear that lady four tables over is waving a no-way-don't-worry-about-it towards your table.

"You know, I bet you're right. It was nice meeting you guys."

"What a peculiar woman," Shelia states before Ambyrr is completely out of earshot. You can hear Ambyrr's nervous laughter push out as she sits next to her mother.

And as you sit, you're unsure of what to do with the wrinkled hands extended to either side of your plate. Taking Matthew's nodding prompt, you grasp the hands and lower your eyes. Clinton begins speaking:

"Oh Blessed Lord, Oh Dearest Virgin; we ask that you bless this food to the nourishment of our bodies and of all mankind...."

Prayer. Your cue to relax your forced smile and use the moment to take in the men and women surrounding you. You let your eyes lock on Clinton first, his lips barely opening as he exudes praises on the Lord Almighty. His salt-and-pepper hair is combed over a growing bald spot at his crown, locked in place by too-little pomade so that the air conditioning blows wisps of it about. You wonder if he planned it that way, with his seat directly in the rays pouring through the blinds, catching light on his waving hair like one of those halos in the Renaissance paintings.

To your right Claudette's double chin triples as she forces her eyes down to her plate. Her hands struggle to not fidget in the grasp of Gayle and Matthew; not to reach toward the rolls and mashed potatoes, well-done steak and dried out-chicken breast, creamed corn, green beans, and bacon-fat black-eyed peas. As Clinton continues to beg his God for an apparently non-automatic blessing, Claudette's plate becomes holier and holier, fighting hard to outshine every plate in the place.

You manage to close your eyes just before the table counters Clinton's "amen" and smile broadly as each of your Catholic instructors begin eating silently, glancing around and deftly avoiding your eyes.

"So, you come here every Sunday?" you ask.

"Just about," Pat responds, smiling. "We always manage to meet up somewhere after mass. Speaking of which, did you enjoy the service?"

Pat's eyes sparkle with a sincerity you'd thought obsolete before. Or at least saved for stories about Santa Claus. He forks in a mouthful of green beans and glances over toward Matt.

And sometimes, silence is awkward.

"Thank you all for having me along," you say. "I don't want to be a burden. Please, carry on as you normally would. I'm sure I can get the information I need from your typical conversation."

"He's writing a dissertation on the communal religious ideology of various congregations throughout the city."

Mark must have told Matt this.

"It's for my humanities class at school."

More silence and chewing. You swear that every table in the restaurant is hanging on your conversation.

"I'm sure anything you guys have to discuss will work. So just fire away."

And still no one answers you. After what seems like an eternity, Gayle finally pipes up:

"Do you believe in our Lord and Savior Jesus Christ?" she asks, and you choke on your chicken breast. You know nothing you can say right now is going to be the correct answer. A "yes" would lead to expounding. A "no" would shut them up completely. A "maybe." Well, that would just not be acceptable. So instead, you smile.

"I believe that He existed. And that He was a very great man."

"Oh, but He was more than just 'man'," Gayle says, "He is both God and Man. That's what makes Him so wonderful. He died for all our sins and is now up in Heaven with his father, our Heavenly Father, looking out for us all."

"He's kind of like the mediator between us and God," Matt explains. "Since Jesus was human, he understands our plight, our evil ways...."

"And our good," Claudette pipes in.

"Exactly," Matt continues with an intense look in your direction. "Jesus understands us. He is there for us. That is why he created the Catholic Church. Jesus appointed the first Pope, you know."

Everyone at the table is all smiles at this point. Either they've relaxed, or they're pompous. Or maybe both.

"Do you have any questions?"

This is not something you are expecting to be asked. But you do have questions. As omnipotent as you may be, there are always things you cannot wrap your head around. And so they pour out:

Why would Jesus need to be a mediator between God and humans if the Father, the Son, and the Holy Spirit are all one and the same? And if they're not —if they each have separate facets and knowledge— how does that support a monotheistic religion? And what does it mean to be "born again"? And after you're "born again" can you just sin away and, as long as you ask for forgiveness and say a couple-a "Hail Mary"s, be A-OK in the afterlife?

And to your surprise, despite your barrage of questions, your company is still smiling and seem completely ready and willing to answer you. To spread the word of God.

Clinton explains that one of the Catholic's Spiritual Works of Mercy is to "instruct the ignorant." The ignorant in this case being you. So you sit back and wait to be enlightened. The merciful being the old man who adjusts his glasses and purses his lips as your words spew forth, the old woman who ignores your barrage to focus on her plate.

And so you learn about the Nicene Creed. How God was there and He was unable to leave Heaven to come to Earth —to which you want to interject, but just decide to keep your mouth shut— so he projected himself in the form of the Holy Spirit down to Mary and made Jesus. Made Jesus from himself. But not in that clay/rib way from Genesis. God had evolved past that. Although not in the Darwin sense of the word. That would just be preposterous.

At any rate, nowadays, God and Jesus are together in Heaven but are fully one in the same since Jesus was made from, not begot of, God. And the Holy Spirit is... Well, if Ambyrr were here, she'd say it is like God's astral body.

To be "born again" is to be baptized.

And finally, although God is loving and Jesus died for our sins and is waiting to welcome us into Heaven, confession and contrition are not the answers to everything. Catholics still try to love a holy life. The reason for confession is that God knows we are imperfect. That's why he sent his only son.

"But as long as we hold in mind the Cardinal Moral Virtues of prudence, justice to others, temperance, and fortitude...."

"And as long as we cherish our faith, hope, and love for ourselves and mankind...."

"God will accept us in His open embrace for all of eternity."

You have to admit, that's one hell of a consolation prize for a lifetime of deterrence from moral ambiguities.

"Should we load back into the van?" Matt asks, surprising you. You, omnipotent you, so wrapped up in your learning you fail to even notice the meal ending.

"I can just take the bus back to my place from here," you say. "It's not very far at all. It was a pleasure talking with all of you."

"It's no problem at all, dear," Sheila says, patting your shoulder as she heads for the door.

"It was very nice to meet you." Pat.

"Come back and visit the Church anytime." Clinton.

"You know, dear," Gayle whispers into your ear as she walks by. "According to the Word of God, sodomy is a sin which cries to Heaven for vengeance."

The students from the medical program at Emory all drink Earl Grey. They think it makes them seem scholarly. You enjoy this because all you have to do is scoop leaves into a strainer and pour hot water into a mug. You hate this because you, omnipotent you, know that means a tip of exactly twenty-six cents: the change from two dollars.

The kids from Tech all want a shot-in-the-dark or a red-eye or whatever fancy name they can give to a doppio in a medium cup of coffee. You charge $3.85 for a shot-in-the-dark, $3.15 for a red-eye. They never catch on.

The liberal arts seekers from State all want a macchiato and, when you're in a good mood, you'll explain that Starbucks has no clue what a macchiato really is and, when you're not, you give them their shot of espresso with their dollop of foamed milk. Just to watch them try to sip it down.

Tonight, you're not in a good mood. Tonight you're too distracted by Mark. Mark sitting on the patio chain smoking. Mark tapping the window between customers to remind you of your open notebook. Mark. Mark who says: Remember to write.

You left for work an hour early today. You snuck out with cash in your shoe and eighteen DV tapes in the bottom of your messenger bag. You left early so you had time to stop by the Mega Mart for a TV/VCR deal and an adapter cassette. The cheapest one they had was a twelve-inch hot pink number with bright yellow flowers and the mug of a steak-lipped Muppet.

"It's for my sister," you told the cashier who was too wrapped up with the conversation she was having with Line 12 B to even notice what you were purchasing.

Now, it's set up in the break room with Tape 1 inserted and ready. And Mark. Mark is smirking at you as if he knows you're just dying to get back there to start viewing what Mabel left behind.

Instead you decide on a compromise and join Mark on the patio for a cigarette.

"You just hanging out to make sure I'm rewriting the Bible?"

"Is that hostility in your voice?" Mark asks with the sweetest demeanor he can summon. With the slightest hint of laughter he can manage. "I just enjoy your company. You just have such a sweet face."

You concede a smirk and plop into the plastic chair beside your roommate.

"Matt called earlier," Mark says, offering you his baby blue lighter. "He told me you were quite inquisitive during your lunch."

"Yeah...."

"He hopes you'll join them again for another service."

You light your cigarette and hold your breath.

"I'm not your keeper." Mark says this as if you should actually believe it. "It's completely up to you who you spend your time with."

Mark slides an ashtray across the table for you. "As long as you keep writing."

"I've got a customer," you mumble and hand Mark your half-smoked cigarette as you move to the door.

"Hey," Mark smiles. "After work, let's run by the store. I think we should dye your hair tonight."

twenty two

Mark is standing in his underwear. In tight black boxer briefs and off-white latex gloves. And you. Your underwear is white and barely peaking into the mirror.

The bathroom is way too small for two people. Its black and white tiled walls, the red and black skull-and-crossbones shower curtain, they weren't designed for a group hair dying session. So Mark. Mark has to press tight against you as he shakes up a bottle of Nice 'N Easy 105, breaks the tip, and decides you're going to look much better with black hair. Mark presses tighter than he really needs to.

You stare into the mirror as Mark moves around you, squirting black gel into his hand and spreading it over your scalp. Moving up from the root to the tip of your hair. Paying close attention at your neckline and around your ears.

Mark tells you the dye needs to sit and develop for about twenty minutes. That's what the box says. Twenty minutes. But he always gives it about an hour.

Mark says, while it's developing you can't lean against the wall. You can't lie down. You probably shouldn't sit on the couch in case it drips down. You probably shouldn't go into your bedroom, as white as it is in there.

Mark says, "Why don't you just come up to my room?"

In the months you've known Mark, in all the nights and afternoons and mornings he's spent in your bed, in all this time, you've never seen into Mark's room. Mark. His room is up a narrow flight of stairs off the kitchen. Stairs that look like they were added later. Like leftovers from a secret hideout during the Underground Railroad. Like Harriet Tubman built them herself.

And when you enter, you are honestly expecting more. You look around at the Spartan furnishings. A single bed. Several metal bookshelves, painted black, packed full with books. History books. Some of which look older than the ones they're still using at the public schools. And religious books. Bibles. The Koran. Every edition. Every version. Books by Nietzsche, by LaVey, by Crowley. A collection that must have taken years. Decades. Eons.

Mark watches you admire the spines.

He says, "I do my own research." Mark. He says, "Sit down."

You pull out the rolling chair from his desk as he sits on a trunk at the foot of his bed.

"Did Clara tell you about the *tikum alum*?"

And here's Mark. The teacher. Mark who tells you about the Jewish idea that at the dawn of time, in that world of creationism, a vessel held all of the light of the world. And because the light was so great, because it could not be contained, because some idiot fell on top of it, the vessel shattered and all of the light escaped. Disbursed. Permeated the ozone layer and drilled little tiny holes to let in all the ultra-violent rays. Cosmic sunburning.

The job of the Jew, Mark says, is to put the pieces of the jar back together. That mankind is responsible to each get themselves a bottle of rubber cement and try to glue as many shards back on as possible. Every good deed uncovers a part of the puzzle. Every good deed is a *tikum alum*.

"If it helps," Mark says, Mark as mentor says, "that's what you're doing. What you're writing. Your words are going to repair the vessel. Put the lid back on the jar."

"Leave the world in utter darkness."

Mark smirks. His stone grey irises are almost drowned out by his pupils as the muscles in his face contract. Mark's smile framed by black stubble.

Mark smirks and says, "If something is devoid of light, does that necessarily mean it's dark?" Mark. He smirks and says, "You should probably hop in the shower and wash the dye out of your hair." He says, "I think you're going to look sexy in black."

twenty three

Some people are just sexier in memory. That's the way it is with Muambwo. That's what Mark says. Mark says when you're with him, he's alright, but once he's gone you start to really understand how enticing his brown-black eyes are, how much you get really turned on by his lips.

Mark. He tells you this in your morning-after bed and you suddenly find yourself extremely conscious of your nude body and missing sheets.

Mark rolls to his side and kisses your shoulder before propping his head up on his hand. He's angling for your eyes.

"I think you'll really like him," Mark says. "Just don't call him Justin."

"Why would I call him Justin?"

"Well, that's his real name. His 'white slave name.' He changed it to Muambwo in search of his African roots or whatever. He was born in Wyoming. Anyway. I used to like to give him a hard time about it."

You roll to your side, smashing your cheek into the residue of the black dye your new hairdo has left on your pillow.

"So how did you meet Muambwo?"

Mark is silent. Smirking.

"He used to be really into voodoo culture."

Mark says this as if it's an explanation. Mark says, "Before you meet him though, I think you need to spend some more time with Harry. I'll give Harry a call to make sure he'll be around. Call into work tomorrow."

You flash to the hot pink TV and Mabel's tapes waiting in the break room of The Morning Bean.

Mark smirks and climbs over you and out of the bed.

twenty four

Every writer has a god-complex. That's why every main character thinks he's god. If it were up to you though, this time the main character would have a little more say over the who, the where, the when. If it were up to you, you'd be telling Haripreet that, although you'd given a lot of consideration to the words he'd spoken, you didn't feel quite ready for the makeover you are about to receive.

But it's not up to you.

"I'm so ecstatic that you've agreed to the *shuddhikaran*."

And you believe him.

"Please remove your clothing."

The fluorescent light in the kitchen beats out the flicker of tiny flames, dozens of them, spread around the living room. They all fight for a one-man-show reflection in the barber straight razor as Haripreet approaches you for your really close shave.

You. You're sitting in the lotus position atop a few white towels Harry must have picked up at the Bed, Bath, and Beyond for this occasion. You're trying hard to keep your mind clear, your face serene. To keep your third eye open. Not to pick at the terry cloth next to your knees.

"Have you done this before?"

"Don't worry. Clear your mind. You're in good hands."

Haripreet tells you to focus on the flame of the candle directly in front of you. The one burning down quickly and depositing white wax on the entertainment center. He gives you a mantra. To chant internally, with your inner voice, so you don't move your head.

He tells you not to close your eyes as he dips the razor into a white ceramic bowl of water and kneels down behind you.

Your own chant is a little more vain. Wondering if you'll look good bald. You're trying to keep your face serene, keep your third eye open, figure out why Mark dyed your hair only to send you to Harry for this makeover.

The razor is cold against your scalp. You could imagine it as soothing if it weren't for the hair ripping at its roots. You try to withhold a grimace Haripreet could easily see reflected in his television screen.

But Harry is in a world of his own. His voice is low as he chants. His hands move quickly and efficiently over your scalp.

You read up on this before you came over tonight. Not on the *shuddhikaran*. But on shaving your head. Apparently Haripreet did not.

You're supposed to trim your hair as close as possible before you pull out the razor. Your hair is supposed to be really wet to minimize discomfort. You're supposed to use shaving cream.

At least Harry is using some sort of oil on your hair to make it easier to cut.

Haripreet drops the razor into the ceramic bowl and you exhale deeply with the clank. He continues to chant as he coats your scalp in more oils. Your eyes are watering. The scent of sandalwood is overpowering. You want water. You try to focus on Haripreet's words.

"*Om Navah Shivaye. Om Sadyojaatam...*"

You smell milk and honey and scents you can't quite place. Your head feels sticky. You can feel dollops of something fall to your shoulders.

Haripreet wraps your head in fabric and sits directly in front of you, falling into the lotus position gracefully. You expect him to finish his chant and smile. Instead his eyes look into you, past you, and his lips continue to move as if on motor-function reflex. You try to look serene. You try to open up your third eye and stare right back in his direction.

You sit for an hour more and try not to fall asleep.

You stretch your eyelids as wide as you can while Haripreet rises to his feet, still lost in his Mantras. He unwraps your head. In the reflection of the television screen you see him lift a white porcelain pitcher.

The water is freezing as it pushes over your scalp. You hope the gasp and jerk in your shoulders go unnoticed. You bite your tongue and hold your breath.

And then again the sandalwood. Harry is spreading a thick paste to form a thin layer over your scalp.

"*Bhave Bhavenaati Bhave Bhavasvamaam Bhavodbhavay Namah....*"

The smell is intoxicating. More so than when the incense overwhelmed you the first time you visited. It clouds your eyes. Even your third eye can no longer make out the eight armed goddess perched on the bookshelf beside the entertainment center. The bells around her seem coated with a thin film. The skulls at her feet stare blindly forward. They can't make out a thing either.

"*Namo Rudraay, Namah Kaalay, Namah Kala....*"

Harry is wiping away the paste. You feel it dripping to your bare shoulders, down your back, your chest. Harry adeptly brushes it away and you are clean, refreshed. Naked. And Harry. He is on his feet, dancing around you. He holds a bell in one hand, a cone of incense in the other. Incense embraced in a golden temple. He is nearly singing.

You. You are longing for some sense of time. For something other than glimpses that reach into you. You, omnipotent you, want an understanding. You feel Haripreet touching your scalp. You notice the feel of his skin, how even though it's smooth and uncalloused it pulls at your freshly exposed scalp in places where the oil dries. You're sure Haripreet has a papercut on the ring finger of his left hand. You notice the air blowing over your crown. Saffron. You ears. You hear sounds as if you are a mile away. As if Harry is covering your head with a pillowcase.

"How do you feel about death?"

You open your eyes. The dream state is gone. The *dhoop*, the saffron, the sandalwood. Gone. Your eyes focus on Haripreet.

His smile lines are sharp and he shovels rice from a takeout box into his mouth. His eyes are bright with the overhead light. The candles are snuffed out and put away.

"Do you want some?" Harry asks, still nude in front of the television, extending the Styrofoam container of curry toward you. "My fast is finally over. I am starving."

You take a moment to stretch out of the lotus position, catch a glimpse of your clothes folded neatly at your side, and quickly grab them to cover yourself.

"You're welcome to dress yourself if you would like."

You excuse yourself into the kitchen and pull back into your clothing. You cannot resist rubbing the top of your head. Feeling the new bare skin stick and pull from your palm. You fumble for a toaster or spoon, trying to catch a reflection anywhere.

Haripreet joins you on the linoleum floor, tossing his fork into the sink. He puts the curry on the counter and grabs a banana.

"The *shudihkaran* suits you."

Thanks. You smile. You are still the pupil. The newly baptized lesser mortal in the presence of the guru. The guru with the mouth full of potassium.

"When did your fast end?"

"When the ritual ended. I, myself, am not wholly pure. Therefore I must fast. I must give penance in order to purify you. I, myself, must become as close to holy as I may be granted by the gods before I can impart their love, their wisdom onto you."

You think of Matthew. Confession before Communion. Of Ambyrr, asking permission and forgiveness before she picks a sprig of basil from her garden. You smile.

"You are truly righteous," Haripreet continues. "Your smile, it is infectious. Even before the ceremony I sensed it in you. That love. That desire. That inability to cause harm. That, my friend, is essential to our faith. We embrace all people. We want harm to none. Even those who do not believe in the true faith."

Again you smile. Haripreet smiles. He takes another bite from his fruit.

"Are you sure I cannot offer you anything to eat?"

Suddenly you are aware of your stomach growling.

"How long was I out?"

And again with the smiling. Your cheeks are beginning to throb and quiver as you force them wider and wider.

"You were in your trance for several hours. Welcoming in our gods. They were reaching into you, enlightening you. You are most well-received."

Haripreet offers you an orange and moves a small sugar ant from the fruit bowl to the window, shooing it through the screen. Harm to no living creature.

"You are not like so many others who become entranced by our gods. Those who seek only to act as sightseers, as if our ways are a sideshow. Those who attempt to make a mockery of our gods. Those men who are *Asuras.* Those who deserve death for failing to embrace the feelings of the true believers."

Harm to none.

You stop trying to peel the orange and hand it back to your host, your guru.

"I should probably be getting home. I'm sure it's late. Mark's probably waiting for me."

Harm to none.

twenty six

"What the fuck happened to your head, son? You look like one of them cancer ward kids the third graders around here are always doing math problems for."

Your hand instinctively flies to your scalp. Already you can feel the heat exuding from your skin in waves, as if all this time it's just been waiting to burn in the crisp Georgia air. You feel sickly. You've started avoiding mirrors.

Mark winks at you from the beer cooler as he grabs a couple cases and heads toward the door. Leonard waves him on through, jotting himself a note to accidentally erase the security footage from three fifteen until three thirty-two.

"Betty Ann really enjoyed having you boys over to the house for dinner," Leonard continues, rounding the counter and tapping out a cigarette. "That's what she told me to say. 'Really enjoyed.' Like the fucking fat cow is some sort of sophisticated society cunt." Leonard lets out his phlegmmy guffaw, squeezing his eyes tight as his face reddens to match your scalp. "Let's grab a smoke. You may wanna take some of that ice blue colored aloe vera shit and rub it up on that dome. Aisle three. Next to the aspirin and cunt rags."

You meander down the QuickSave aisle and pick up the smallest bottle of aloe you can find. Its electric blue dye is offset by the neon yellow and pink promising 'Instant Relief!' and 'An Unbeatable Bargain!' on the packaging. You squeeze a small glob into your hand and wince as you bring it to your scalp.

"Hurry your ass up!" Leonard pokes his head back through the door. "I ain't gone erase the tape for too long. Starts to look fishy."

Mark is sitting on the hood of his car, absently flicking his cigarette and weaving his head to keep his eyes in shadow and avoid the piercing sun. He tosses you his key and you throw the aloe into the passenger seat before joining the father and son pair for a Lucky Strike.

"So I promised you boys I'd tell you about James Raiken the last time you were here. I was gonna tell you when you came over for dinner, but it ain't appropriate dinner conversation according to your bitch momma."

Mark leans back on his hood and shields his closed eyes with his hand. You begin to do the same, and he jabs a finger into your ribcage. You sit back up and look at Leonard earnestly.

"James Raiken; we all called him Buddy. He fell into lockup round about the time I took up death row duty over in Jackson. You ain't going to find his name on any papers though. There ain't a single record of him ever being incarcerated in the state of Georgia, let alone being executed here. If a congregation has enough money, and enough people in the right places, they can keep anyone quiet."

Leonard flicks his smoke once more and squeezes his lips tightly, as if he's tasting his words. As if he savors this anecdote, his part in it. The way it rolls around in his larynx.

"Buddy and his pastor walked into the station house on a Tuesday evening. Buddy walked in with his hands held out and his pastor holding tight to the Holy Bible. Buddy walks right on up to the front counter and he says, 'I done something terrible.'

"I didn't even bother unclipping my pistol. I just looked up at Buddy and I says, 'What terrible thing did you do?' Behind me there was child molesters, rapers, fucking niggers who done shot their best friend from kindergarten over rock. So I look at this white man with sad brown eyes and a receding hairline, this guy with his pastor and his Bible urging him to put his hands down and just tell his story. I look at them both and say, 'What terrible thing did you do?'

"Buddy tells me how his wife and kid are dead. How they been dead for going on three weeks now and ain't nobody gone looking for them 'cause they ain't got no family other than him. How they been dead for three weeks now and that means his daughter, his little baby girl is almost two months old. The man's brown eyes are filling up with tears. Buddy may not be the first man to cry like a fucking woman in the jailhouse, but he was certainly going for the most remorseful. His preacher just goes on holding up his Bible, flashing the gold lettering in the light, trying to blind me or hypnotize me with the word of God.

"'How'd they die, Mr. Raiken?' I asked even though I already knew the answer. I already knew he done offed the both of them and I still knew I didn't need to reach for my gun or my cuffs. Buddy looked at the ground for a long time. His eyes glazed as he stared at the star on my shirt. Finally he tells me he did it. He tells me that at first he didn't remember but he talked to Brother Egan, his pastor, the man standing right there beside him. He talked to Brother Egan and Brother Egan let the Holy Spirit into him, right into Buddy. And Buddy saw what had happened.

"Buddy saw himself come home from the bar drunk. He saw his wife standing there in the kitchen, her back to him, making goo and gaa sounds like some sort of fucking retard. Buddy saw how there weren't no dinner plate waiting for him and he done grabbed the woman by the shoulders and pushed her into the sink. Buddy saw it all in the third person. Like the Holy Spirit had been there watching, trying to stop him, but couldn't interfere because God needed Buddy to learn a lesson. God needed Buddy to come back to Him and that little baby girl flying in slow motion out of her momma's arms was just on her way to meet her Lord and Savoir a little bit early. That little baby girl who had her momma's nose and Buddy's brown hair. She was so slow in coming out of her pink blanket. She was so slow in hitting the linoleum floor next to her momma's bare feet. So slow in bouncing up and down, bashing her tiny soft skull on the wooden table leg. On the table leg that led to the table that had no dinner plate waiting for Buddy. Buddy's wife Glenda screamed and threw herself next to her daughter. She held her and caressed her and tried to get her to drink more from her titty. She cooed and cried. And the whole time Buddy looked and knew his little girl weren't breathing no more. That she weren't breathing no more and it was all his fault and no one knew except his wife Glenda.

"That's when he grabbed for Glenda again. He could say he was sorry, but that wasn't the Lord's plan. Glenda dropped their baby girl as Buddy's hands closed round her neck. Buddy heard another crunching sound and he didn't know if it was the voice box in his wife's throat or the little brittle bones under his work boots.

"Buddy says the Holy Ghost wouldn't show him the next part. He says he can't say for sure how they got there, but if we sent a couple men out to his house on Rosewood Drive we'd surely find his wife's nude body in a shallow grave in his backyard. We'd find his wife's naked body clutching onto a crushed blue baby girl covered in dirt and red clay. Buddy says he ain't no necrophiliac so there ain't no seed in his poor wife's pussy. Buddy says some of the grass has just started growing back where all the dirt got turned over."

Leonard pauses as he throws his cigarette butt under the tire of the Crown Vic rolling into the space next to Mark's car. He nods to the men barreling out and follows them into the convenience store.

You. You sit staring at him rounding the counter to ring up the cola and potato chips the men are placing by the cash register. Mark hands you a beer from his backseat and tells you to go back into the store if you want to hear the rest of the story. He pulls the tab on his can and toasts the men getting back into their car.

Inside Leonard is stocking cigarettes and whistling to himself. He glances over his shoulder as you push through the door. You swallow hard and try not to grimace as the bitter taste of fermented malt rushes down your throat. You put your can on the counter and wait for Leonard to finish whistling his song.

"I ain't never seen a man more broken up about something than James Raiken. I almost felt sorry for the fucker as I led him into a holding cell and hopped in a squad car with Brother Egan to check out Buddy's story. I didn't need to even ask him to go into the cell. But he kept his hands out the whole time like he wanted the handcuffs. Like he wanted me to rough him up and toss his ass onto the cement next to the john in the cell.

"Brother Egan directed me to a little blue house at the end of Rosewood and I parked the cruiser behind a rusted brown shit-trap of a car. I reached for the handle to get out and felt Brother Egan's fist wrap around my forearm.

"'We don't need to go back there,' Brother Egan says. 'James is an astute member of our congregation. He's a drunk, true, but God has a plan, and God works in mysterious ways,' and more of that Biblical mumbo jumbo to make it okay that God's people are fucking fuckups who should be forgiven if they give enough money in the collections plate. Brother Egan looks at me and tells me his congregation can't afford a scandal. He says, 'James is such a respected member of our church and we can't afford to have a scandal. But we can afford a cover up.'"

Leonard leans across the counter, the fluorescent light glowing in his winking eye. He winks you in on the conspiracy. His smirk would mirror Mark's if his face were thinner, less red and wrinkled.

"Brother Egan opened up his Bible, and there in place of the bookmark were two hundred dollar bills. He slammed shut the cover and placed the Bible in my hands.

"'Well, of course I have to offer up a tithe to my church," I says. Brother Egan just stares at me for a moment. He stares and then pulls a twenty out of his wallet. 'I tithe twenty percent,' I says."

Leonard tells you how he drives back to the station. How he leads Brother Egan passed Buddy's cell, the brown haired man sobbing relentlessly in the corner. How Brother Egan makes an offer to the chief, promising a hefty donation to the department as well as a personal donation on the side to help clear up the paperwork. In exchange, Brother Egan wants no investigation. The poor woman had no family other than Buddy anyway. In exchange, Brother Egan wants Buddy to receive his judgment without trial, without press, without any record of him ever being in the jail. In exchange he wants Buddy's wish of a lethal injection to be carried out without the governor knowing, without the news media finding out.

Leonard tells you how the chief looks at the number Brother Egan has scrawled on a scrap of paper and slid across the table. Leonard tells you how it all looks like one of those mob movies, one of those shady underhanded deals you see in the late night black and white movies on TBS. Leonard tells you how the chief considers the number, considers the personal donation, considers his kid's need of braces and a swimming pool with a Jacuzzi. Leonard tells you how the chief nods to Brother Egan and then to Leonard himself. How he leads Brother Egan back to the front, stopping briefly for the pastor to say "may God be with you" to Buddy on his way out the door.

Leonard tells you all this and smiles. He smiles and pulls the shotgun out from under the counter.

He says, "I know I don't have to tell you this 'cause you're Mark's friend and all, but this story– This story is top fucking secret and it don't need to ever get repeated."

You. You consider the gun for a moment and then look Leonard in the eye. You. You say, "How would that ever happen? How would the department be able to cover up an inmate? How could you hide the fact that you've essentially euthanized someone under the guise of the law? I just. That just doesn't happen."

"How the hell do you know? Do you work on fucking death row?" Leonard smiles as he shoves the gun below the counter, nodding toward Mark asleep on the hood of his car. "You boys probably need to get a run on. Next time you're up, I'll tell you about Buddy's time in the cell."

Dress nicely. Wear black. The goal here is to blend in. As much as possible. Mark tells you this as he stands over you. You. You're barely awake and your alarm clock is still creeping slowly toward four am. Mark's head is blocking enough of the overhead light burning to give your eyes a moment to adjust.

"You've got a busy day today. Get ready."

The only thing you know about is work. A shift at The Morning Bean that starts over twelve hours from now.

"I called in for you yesterday," Mark says. "You're still really sick. You may be dying."

Mark is tossing slacks and a button up shirt onto your bed. He pulls out socks and shoes. He lifts the covers to determine if your drawers are white or black. They're plaid.

You barely have your shoes on before Mark is herding you out the door to his car. He's got the car cranked before you've finished pouring yourself into the passenger seat.

"Where are we going?"

Mark smirks. Mark smirks as if you should know better than to ask questions by now. You. You're just along for the ride.

You careen down empty pre-dawn roads. You watch yuppies jogging with pugs, jogging with terriers, crowding the sidewalks before they shower and crowd the roads, heading in for their fluorescent office Friday.

Mark pulls up to a nondescript building. There's no sign delineating it from the other businesses lining to street. Its windows are as dark as those in the surrounding office buildings. The only thing that sets it apart is the small crowd of people slipping through the doorway.

Mark lets the car idle on the street.

"Hop out."

"Are you going to park?"

"You're on your own on this one. Alia will meet you inside. Just find a seat."

You stare numbly at Mark. He reaches over and wipes the sleep from your eyes. He smiles. Mark's smile.

"The service isn't too long then you and Alia will have a bit to talk. After that just hop on the bus for your next appointment. Here's the address." Mark slides a sheet of notebook paper into your shirt pocket and gives you a tap. "You're late already."

You reach for the door handle and pull yourself from the car.

Inside, the building is almost as drab as its exterior. The black and white marble floor tile is dingy and grey, cracked and dulled from years of buffing. Grecian columns holding up nothing in particular stand with none of the elegance the designer had intended. Just beyond the lobby a muddied blue carpet flattens hallways into darkness.

A sign you can't read points down the hall on your left which the brass plate on the lobby wall identifies as the direction of the conference room. You walk down the hallway, wondering what Mark has planned for you.

When you push open the door to the conference room you see row upon row of kneeling figures. The left side of the room is all men; the right side all women. Before you can take a step, two men rush toward you. Their tan faces are intense and it takes you a moment to register their eyes are fearful instead of the angry you expected. They take your shoulder and lead you into the hallway.

"Why are you here?"

Your mind flashes to images of torture, to suitcase bombs. Oil and turbans. You try desperately to hide it from your eyes.

"He's with me."

The two men turn to the pretty Middle Eastern woman who has appeared in the doorway behind them. Her eyes are strong beneath the floral wrap covering her hair. She keeps her jaw steady as she crosses her hands in front of her simple black dress.

The men consider her for a moment before turning back to you. Finally their shoulders go slack as they pat down your pockets like security officers, mumbling an "I'm sure you understand" before letting you go and returning to their posts just inside the conference hall.

Your savoir smiles and introduces herself as Alia. She tells you that everyone's kind of on edge since the country's at war. She tells you they can't even meet in the Mosque on 14th Street right now because of periodic bomb threats, protesters, and thrown Coca-Cola cans. She tells you she's glad you could come. She keeps at least three feet between you both as she nods for you to back further into the hallway.

"You'll have to wait in the hall though," Alia says. "'It is not for such as join gods with Allah, to visit or maintain the mosques of Allah while they witness against their own souls to infidelity.' It's nothing personal, and my dad's pretty forward thinking, but the Qur'an is the Qur'an. I did get him to agree to let you sit in the hallway. And we'll leave the door open."

"Your dad?"

"He leads the *Khotba.* That's him in the front. I'll meet you here as soon as I can."

Alia smiles and nods before returning to the conference room and kneeling near the rear of the women's side of the room.

You let your back slide down the wall and strain to hear through the open doorway. You are fascinated, your mind jumping through a stream of consciousness that simultaneously embarrasses you and empowers you. You see all these veils, all these beards. You watch them bowing in prayer. You see news crews, piles of bodies. You see Alia close her eyes serenely. You see buildings falling and soldiers on all sides ducking for cover. You wonder if the people in your mind have anything at all to do with Islam. You wonder how these people before you connect to it.

twenty eight

"*As-Sal ā mu `Alayka.*"

Alia pulls you out of your trance on the hallway carpeting. Your legs are stiff as you uncross them. You smile up at Alia's brown eyes, her round face. Behind her men and women are coupled again, are walking like friends heading for a Pilates class, are trying not to stare at you from the corner of their eyes as they meander from the conference room and toward the front lobby.

"What does that mean?"

"It means 'may peace be upon you.'" Alia takes a step back as you climb to your feet.

"*As-Sal ā mu `Alayka,*" you smile, struggling with the pronunciation.

"It would actually be *As-Sal ā mu `Alayki* when addressing a female."

You peer past Alia's veil to the portly man behind her. His beard is a rich white made even brighter by his tanned skin. He smiles as he places his hands on his daughter's shoulders.

"Thank you for letting me attend your service. It was very beautiful."

His smile is rich and warm. Next to his white beard his lips curl as if he were Santa Claus, his expansive chest heaving beneath his clothing.

"It looks like we may have a mu'min on our hands," he says to Alia. Then turning to you, "It's nice to be able to show that we're not all about violence and anger. We're also about hating Jews and reclaiming our Holy City."

Your mind flashes to Clara as your face goes slack. His face, Alia's father's face is serious, but the glint in his eye remains, telling you all those words you couldn't understand were not about jihad. You think.

Alia breaks your gaze.

"You want to get some coffee? I know this indie place called The Morning Bean that's pretty good."

You order a triple latte and smirk as you count the shots out long. You would say something, but you're exhausted from your early morning wake up call, and this isn't your coffee shop anyway. Alia luckily agreed to drop by Aurora instead of The Morning Bean, so you decide to take blessings where you can get them.

You ask for a shot of vanilla to combat the bitterness of the short-pulled shots and toss your change into the tip jar before joining Alia at a table beside the window.

"What is it you are searching for?"

Alia's hair is lush and wavy as she removes her hijab and carefully drapes it over the back of her chair. You watch as she runs her hands through her black tresses and vainly suppress a smile as you ponder the ultimacy of her question.

"Isn't that what I should be asking you?"

Alia smiles and sips her coffee. "Shoot."

"Your father. He called me a 'mu'min.' What does that mean?"

Alia explains that the Qur'an delineates between a true Muslim and a believer. That the believer is called a mu'min. That her father sees you as someone whose heart it open to believe but has not yet allowed the faith to enter into your it. Like a Christian without the head dunk. Like the one out of ten dentists who doesn't support the commercial per say, but doesn't deny the toothpaste works. She tells you that faith, *iman*, is the most important part of her theology, that it's mentioned countless times within the sacred texts, so that possessing it puts you in alliance with Allah. She tells you that Allah is the one true God and that Muhammad is His Messenger.

"And you know my father was just joking with you, right? About the violence. He has this thing where he thinks he's a comedian. Like if he plays up a combo of news stories and false stereotypes he can get a show on a second rate cable network."

You. You laugh. "Maybe you can give him some pointers on comedy. You're pretty witty."

Alia blushes and lowers her head demurely.

"I'm not an extremist," she says. "All followers of Islam, of the Divine Name of Rahma, we believe in peace and compassion. I belong to a group of young Muslim women who are all about spreading the word and peace and justice. We haven't even discussed that new pregnancy suit bomb."

"Again with the wit."

Alia. She looks at you stoically, barely batting her eyelashes as she says "I do get terrified that it'll be my cousin or my aunt every time I see a news story about a thwarted terrorist attempt."

"Because they're your family or because their attempt was thwarted?"

"I'm glad you understand my humor," Alia smiles.

You watch as Alia sips her coffee gently and slowly. Her lips part slightly while she speaks, telling you that she and her family understand a sense of faith and modernity. That this is why she can remove her headscarf in public. She says the idea that women are subservient is only true in the sense that women and men are each subservient to Allah, who is merciful. Allah empowered men with greater responsibilities, true, but the ultimate role of all peoples is to serve Allah as a means of connecting to goodness.

"I am not here to try to convert you," she says. "We all have a destination from the moment we are born. And God gives us freewill to make those decisions to ensure we reach that peace. And Satan will try to tempt you. To make you forget. That is why I pray to Allah five times each day, to retain that connection. That is why you do what it is you do. To connect with divinity."

You wonder if you should tell her what you're writing has much less to do with connecting and much more to do with erasing. Or if maybe she thinks Mark is divine.

"I would like you to consider, for a moment, that the Qur'an exists as the work of but one. One messenger transcribing the words handed to him directly from God. This is why Christians and Jews can pick and chose what they feel is important. This is why we cannot. To deny part is to deny the whole.

"And while we embrace all religions as paths, we understand that true faith cannot be so finicky with what its followers chose to believe.

"You have faith in your heart," she tells you. She tells you so that you almost believe it. "It is there and it is shining. Allah smiles upon you."

twenty nine

The bus drops you off in a Forest Park shopping center. You can see the makings of a grocery store, a tanning salon, three nail salons. But you would never know it from the signs. The signs are supposed to be handy with their three languages, but you don't know enough Chinese or Vietnamese to figure out any of the lines or slashes. And your Spanish is rusty.

Mark told you to look for the Virgin Mary in the window as if that would be enough to decipher which door to enter. As if there wouldn't be a Virgin of Guadalupe in every other storefront. As if there wouldn't be one emblazoned on the back window of every white pickup truck in the parking lot, airbrushed onto the hoods and side doors of all the minivans.

You adjust the Fidel Castro styled military hat you've taken to wearing to protect your naked skull from the elements and suddenly feel really awkward as Che Guevara bumper stickers beg you for revolution. You pick the door next to a sea of Mary statuettes, each one glowing a brilliant blue from the ceramic cloaks draping over sacred hearts, over china skin, around praying hands. Directly behind the Marys stands a row of black men draped in white, arms spread like Jesus giving His Sermon on the Mount. The clay dirt at his feet proclaims him as Obatala.

Behind the window, the botanica is claustrophobic. It is a mass of sights and sounds, smells all fighting for your attention. With all of the everyday objects verging upon the metaphysical, you wonder if you've inadvertently stepped back into Ambyrr's sunroom. Every inch of the store begs to hold onto your line of sight, all the while blurring into the items beside it. Seven-day candles burn on every surface. You smell incense. You hear clucking.

"Hello. I help you?"

The woman behind the counter doesn't smile. She barely moves. She stands beside the cash register and angles the tiny television screen to make sure you know there are four closed circuit cameras routed her way. That every inch of the front of her shop is covered. She crosses her arms and stares at you like you're a shoplifter. Or worse yet, a tourist.

You barely get out Muambwo's name before she's yelling something over her shoulder. Her eyes never leave yours and two years of high school Spanish leave you with no clue what she's saying.

Before she's finished speaking, the curtain separating the selling floor from the stock room parts and Muambwo steps through. His ebony skin seems epic, making the stark white of his v-neck t-shirt, his drawstring pants, his solid Converse glow. Short twists of hair push out below his solid white trucker cap and Muambwo absently tugs a budding dread as he smiles at you.

Mark. Mark was right about the lips. Perfectly chapped. Parting for a timid smile.

"I am very pleased to meet you." Muambwo does not extend his hand. Instead, he turns to the woman still eyeing you suspiciously and spouts more Spanish. She grunts and nods. "Please," Muambwo continues, "let us go outside where we will have more room to speak."

Muambwo leads the way to the side of the strip mall, rounding the corner and standing between the building and a row of pine trees separating this shopping center from the next. He sighs deeply as he pulls a cigarette from his pocket, lighting it and nodding in your direction as you do the same. He is careful not to lean against the building. Careful not to step into the spots of red clay patchworking the grass.

"I really admire your quest." His voice is less formal now. Now he's speaking to you like you're old friends. Like the two of you really are in your early twenties. "Mark tells me you've really gotten OCD with the whole religion thing."

You. You smile and nod. Although you're not too sure that it's you who is the obsessive compulsive one.

"I've really been on a Don Quixote kick too. Back in Wyoming, I started got into thinking about my ancestors. I fell in with the whole Bob-Marley-taking-back-my-African-roots-mon thing. I'm sure Mark told you I changed my name from Justin to Muambwo."

You smile as he laughs. You stare at the multicolored beaded necklaces wrapped around his throat. You try to make out the patterns of each strand. How many red and black beads there are before it repeats. Where he found brown beads in that shade.

"My name's changing again soon too." Muambwo winks at you conspiratorially. "As soon as my Iagwo period is finished, and I can wear something other than white."

Muambwo is laid back as he tells you the strict rules around his initiation into Santeria. Or rather Lucumi. He says that often the names are synonymous with those who don't understand the faiths. How one begot the other and then found God in its bastardization. He talks about the slave trade and conformation and a subsequent conformity back onto vague ideas of originality.

He tells you how his head was shaved and you blush as his eyes dart around your hat. He tells you how he is only allowed to wear white. How his diet is changed. How he can't eat at a table with others. How eleven months in the system seems on autopilot for him.

"I hated having my head shaved," he admits, again leaning toward you as if he shouldn't be saying it at all. As if he's letting you in on a secret the gods would not have already known. "But purity is important when you are welcoming the gods. And it's growing back fast enough."

"If you have to wear all white, what's with the candy raver action going on around your neck?"

"These are elekes. Each strand represents a god. I wear them for guidance and protection."

You nod and lean back against the dirty white cinder blocks that make up the side of the building. You are surprised at how low-key Muambwo is being. How he's not forcing his rituals on you. How he's not even attempting to convert you. What Mark's comments about his sexiness mean. How you can simultaneously feel rage and jealousy and a desire to go out with the man for a beer.

"So what brought you here?"

"My mom and dad divorced, and my mom decided to move to be closer to her parents. I mostly just wanted out of Wyoming. But it's good. After I got here, I got really into Louisiana-styled Voodoo. So many people were transplanted here after the hurricane and it really opened my eyes to a lot of things. And from the Loa to the islands, I found out more and more about Santeria and it just felt right. And that was the steppingstone to Lucumi and Africa. I'm not going to be so presumptuous as to say it's the one true religion or anything like that. But the gods felt right to me. The stories. The worship. What time is it?"

Muambwo invites you back into the shop. He says not to worry about Maria; she's a really nice lady, just suspicious. He says he's got some work to do in the back room anyway so the two of you will be holed up away from her. He says while he's working he can't really talk much or as candidly as he can outside, but you may find what he's doing interesting.

Inside you try to smile as you scoot passed Maria into the rear of the shop. The clucking sound is louder and you notice seven chickens bobbing their heads inside stainless steel cages. Muambwo smiles.

"We generally sell them as sacrificial offerings," he says. "But we also have to make ends meet so occasionally they become actual dinner instead of magic. You might want to stand back."

Muambwo reaches into a cage and deftly maneuvers his hands around the neck of a white hen. His grip is firm as he pulls the bird into the open air, jerking it quickly above his head, creating a clean snapping sound. Even with her neck broken, the hen continues to flap wildly sending a flurry of feathers onto the floor, exciting the other chickens still bobbing their heads in their cages.

As the movement stops, Muambwo lays the white bird out on the floor, stretching her neck and picking up a small hatchet to remove the head. He holds the bird upside down and lets the fluids from her body pour into a large wooden bowl. The blood is thick, but flows quickly, splashing drops onto the table. Spraying up onto Muambwo's white t-shirt.

Muambwo groans as he lays down the bird and pulls on his shirt to examine the spotting. He takes off his trucker cap, placing it carefully on a clear table. He pulls the t-shirt over his head and wraps it in a plastic bag before digging through a duffle bag for a replacement.

You try not to stare at the small of his back. At his abs as he turns around, donning an identical tee without the red flecks.

"The one thing about having to wear all white," he says, "is that it's so hard to keep clean. I think I'm single-handedly keeping Hanes in business right now."

thirty

"Welcome home, dear."

Mark is using his best Donna Reed. You drop your bag on the floor beside the sofa and wind back into the kitchen.

"What are you cooking?"

"I thought I'd roast a chicken," Mark smiles. He smiles as if he knows what you've just seen. "We're having company for dinner. Do you mind doing the dishes?"

"Who's coming?"

"It's a surprise."

Mark's still smiling. Smirking. Stirring a pot of peas, mashing boiled potatoes. He moves in a choreographed dance around the stove behind you, ensuring that you catch him out of the corner of your eye every time you rinse a spoon. He's reveling.

"You were right about Justin," you say. You're trying to get a reaction. "He is way hotter in memory."

"Muambwo," he corrects you.

Mark corrects you and says, "How'd he like your hair?"

Mark sends you to your room to write. To write until dinner. *Power will always win over creativity.*

"Nietzsche," Mark says, "was a child."

You want to write. You want this entire project to be finished. You want your hair to grow back, to stop staring at the stark white walls of your room. To disprove god. In some sort of context outside of your current situation.

You want someone to answer the door.

As soon as you enter the living room, you're thrown off-guard. The grey army trunk you use as a coffee table is pushed up against the wall behind the door. In its place, two small folding tables are positioned end to end.

"Not quite a banquet hall, but it'll do," Mark says, peeking out of the kitchen doorway. He's using his good-boy voice. The one he only uses when he's introducing you to the people he's set up for you to meet. If he bothers to introduce you. "Do you mind getting the door?"

There are handwritten placards leaning against the ten glasses on the table. Mark's handwriting on lined four by six index cards. Leaning against each of the cups except one.

You catch "Ambyrr Lytte-Prism" on one of the cards as you pass to answer the door.

"What took you so long?"

"I'm sorry, Doct— uh, Clara. I was in the other room."

"I brought some wine. It's kosher."

You take the bottle of Francois Labet white and offer Dr. Goldstein a seat on the couch. "I'll go get Mark."

When you place the wine on the kitchen counter Mark smiles.

"That must be Clara."

You're waiting for some explanation.

"You should probably go entertain her."

Clara's legs are crossed at her ankles. Her hands are clasped in her lap. She's refusing to show her perfect teeth as you pull out the folding chair at the head of the table. The one without the placard.

"So, how have you been?"

"Things at the office have been pretty hectic. Otherwise lovely."

And you're spent. This is as far as you can offer on entertainment.

"I can flip on the TV."

"I'm fine. You don't have to try to amuse me. How's your paper going?"

The one Mark told her you were writing for class.

"Well. I— I'm about halfway through it."

"Isn't school over for the semester?"

"I got an extension."

You can feel Mark's smirk from the other room.

"I'd love to read it when you're finished."

And Mark piles on yet another project for you to undertake. And all you can say is "sure."

"Would you care to take my coat?"

The knock at the door is persistent on first push. Its rapid-fire force tells you who it is before you can even stand.

Mark sweeps into the room, wiping his hands on a charcoal and black plaid apron. He beats you to the door and swings it open.

"Oh my goddess, Mark! Everything smells so good in here! Well, everything except maybe the chicken." Ambyrr laughs, but you'd swear her eyes glazed at the mention of the fowl, that that glint on her lips is drool. "I'm so pleased you invited me tonight! Oh! And look who I ran into while I was walking over — Matt! I saw the blue van parked out front and knew it was either a Catholic or a child molester!"

Ambyrr nudges Matthew Brohmer in his gut as he steps through the doorway, removing his hat. Mark takes the empty Starbucks cup from Ambyrr and tells the guests that you will take their coats.

"There isn't much room on the couch, but if you want to find the index card with your name on it, you can go ahead and sit down at the table. We should be ready shortly."

"Mmmm. Fancy," Ambyrr squeals, locating her seat.

You place the coats on your bed with Clara's. You never thought Carl Jung's Death would seem so welcoming.

one thirty

"Hi. I'm Jude."

You're standing on the front porch smoking when a woman walks up and extends her hand. You toss your cigarette butt into the beer bottle ashtray on the porch railing and meet her handshake. Her grip is firm. Her hands are soft. She has pale white skin that shows no sign of ever aging beyond her mid-twenties. But her eyes. Her eyes are deep with understanding swimming in pale green irises. Her thin lips match her nail polish perfectly. It's a shade of red you only see on soft porn stars.

She smiles as you finish your handshake and pulls her long white-blond hair up into a ponytail, deftly twisting a band from her wrist to hold it into place.

"I'm an old friend of Mark's."

Your eyes trace along the simple gold chain around her neck leading down to the tiny cross. It is perfectly smooth and polished, as if no one had ever been nailed atop it.

You smile as you open the door and lead Jude into the party.

"Jude! I'm so glad you could make it."

Mark is in the living room with the rest of the guests. He is pouring the wine Clara brought into crystal, stemmed glasses you never even knew were in the house. Your eyebrows tense in his direction as he twists his lips upward. His eyes glint from the overhead light bouncing off the spinning blades of the ceiling fan, off the triangular etchings of crystal, and says, "My grandmother gave them to me when I moved out on my own. She may be a hick, but she believes in a good dinner party."

Mark offers Jude a glass of wine as she takes a seat at the placard bearing her name. Clara is already halfway down her glass. Matthew takes his wine and tries desperately to position himself out of Ambyrr's direct line of sight. You can't help but laugh as you sympathize with his disdain at Ambyrr's perpetual diatribe.

"No wine for me," she says. "Do you have on a pot of coffee?"

"I'll put one on," you offer and dive into the kitchen.

You try desperately not to think about the holy war waiting to happen in the living room. You try not to think it odd that all of these people are here. That they all have a different story as to why they met you. That none of them- not Haripreet, not Alia, not Muambwo- none of them needed an introduction to the others as they arrived.

You smirk as you wonder if God or god is the unnamed guest of honor. If Mark has finally gone insane.

You push the brew button on the coffee pot and grab a beer from the refrigerator.

Mark waltzes in and pulls biscuits from the oven.

"It's good that you get to meet Jude tonight," Mark says. "She's the treasurer at the Presbyterian church up near my parents' house. We used to go there before my parents went all insane and thought tongues and snakes were a closer way of reaching into the heart of some fictional jackass.

"I mean, don't tell Jude I said that. Anyway. I've got you scheduled to interview her for your book on Wednesday night. But this is a good way to get the introductions out of the way, right?"

You suppress a laugh as you look at Mark in his plaid apron and oven mitt, holding the tray of biscuits. *Your* book. The one inside of you already. Your biblical reinvention.

"I'm supposed to work Wednesday night. I've already missed too many shifts this month."

"Don't worry. I'll take care of it." Mark smirks. His left cheek tensing his eye into a wink. Into a wink he knows you can't say no to.

"This is all a little weird, don't you think? All these people hanging out together in our living room?"

Mark laughs.

"It's just dinner."

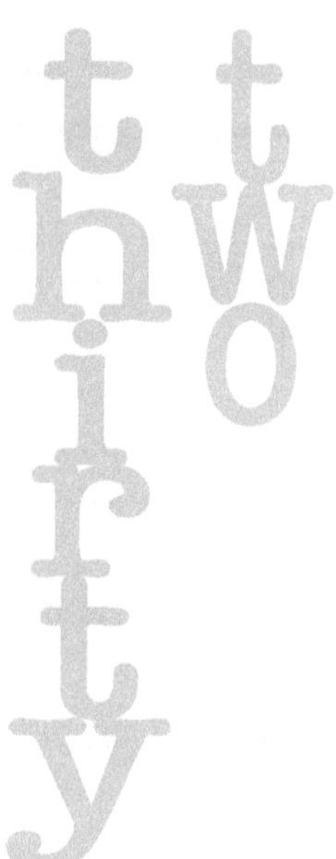

Mark. Mark must have taken sensitivity training at UC Berkley in the '60s. Not that that would have been possible. Not that Mark cares about sensitivity.

But as you take your seat at the end of the table, opposite the unmarked guest of honor chair, you wonder what sort of jihad Mark has in mind.

To your immediate left sits Mark. Of course he's got Muambwo directly to his other side. The Santero is beside the Catholic who is beside the Protestant. Cuba meets Ireland. Ireland torn apart. But neither Matt nor Jude is Irish. And Muambwo is from a book. Justin is from Wyoming.

On the other side of the table is Haripreet, next to you. Still smiling at his reflection on your oiled and sunburned scalp, through the thin stubble beginning to push its way through your skin. Ambyrr is beside him. Then a Muslim. Then a Jew.

And while you're waiting for the mystery man to arrive, you, omnipotent you, are wondering what belief systems will flair. Who's going to start the "walked into a bar" jokes?

Mark smirks.

You should be taking notes.

But no one except Ambyrr is speaking.

The door swings open and a black duffel bag flies into the room, followed by porcelain skin and jet black hair.

"Sorry I'm late. I was wrapping my wigs in toilet paper."

"Welcome home, Mabel," Mark proclaims proudly, not even looking toward the door. All the while staring in your direction.

And everyone in the room says her name. Not like a chant, but it may as well be.

The shock on your face tells Mabel you have yet to watch her tapes. She smiles at you and pours her Lycra biking shorts, her tight black tank top into her chair.

"Let's eat," she smiles and lifts her glass to you.

You brace yourself. You wait for Matt or Jude or Clara to initiate a ring of hands around the table. For prayer.

Instead you see eyes lower, lips moving, hands waving over food, to the forehead, the stomach, each shoulder.

You watch carefully as dishes are passed around the table. Your eye catches the light from the knife as Matthew Brohmer adeptly carves the plump chicken and doles out slabs of meat. For the first time all night Ambyrr is not speaking. Instead her eyes are down trying desperately not to watch the bird being mutilated. She tries in vain to suppress a nervous giggling as Matthew finishes slicing the meat and Mark takes the tray into the kitchen to clear up some room on the table.

You notice that Muambwo is careful not to touch anyone's hands as they pass bowls of salad and mashed potatoes his way. He nods courteously as he passes them onward, not selecting a portion for himself.

Ambyrr asks to ensure none of the vegetables passed to her are cooked in bacon grease or lard. She reads the label on the salad dressing before pouring a small portion over the greens flooding her plate.

"Are you in the middle of a fast, Muambwo?" Haripreet asks. "I just completed one myself." He beams in your direction. You can feel his pupils desperately trying to lock onto your third eye as he smiles into your scalp.

"No, I intend to eat," Muambwo smiles. "I just am not allowed to eat with others for another three weeks." Until his Iagwo period concludes. Until his name changes once again.

"You're welcome to take a plate into the kitchen," Mark smiles at Muambwo. His Donna Reed smile.

"Maybe a little later. Right now, I'd rather enjoy the conversation. And welcome Mabel back."

"Here, here," Mabel laughs and lifts her glass of wine upward. The dinner guests join her toast and you find yourself kicking back almost half your bottle of beer before returning it to the table.

You don't know what is making you so nervous. You know that a multitude of religions is not going to tear your living room apart. Yet Mark. Mark with his smug grin and forkful of mashed potatoes. Mark with his meaningful glance and raised eyebrows. Mark wants a holy war. But not until you finish your book.

You take another swig from your beer, finishing it off and rising to get another from the kitchen. You make sure no one else needs one before disappearing from the room.

You catch your breath and grab a dark green bottle.

In the living room you can hear the clamor of silverware and plates, of people complimenting Mark on his culinary prowess, people telling Mabel it's so good to see her again.

You. You assure yourself it's no big deal, grab a backup beer, and return to your seat.

Mark smirks as you place your opened bottle on the table, your spare on the floor beside the leg of your chair. He nudges your knee. You take the prompt.

"I wanted to thank you guys for all helping me out with this thing I'm writing."

Five years later, you would swear it was a peaceful dinner. You'd swear the conversation seemed planned. Carefully chosen words. Scripts. Five years ago was different. Tonight. Tonight is different.

"It really is a pleasure to speak with you," Haripreet smiles from your side. "I am very pleased with your willingness and openness in learning."

"All religions are really very similar," Ambyrr says. "Faith is faith."

Alia smiles and nods at Ambyrr. You swear she mouths the word "mu'min" as she forks a bite of salad from her plate. But Ambyrr. Ambyrr is never one to just close her mouth.

"As long as you remember that Wicca is the oldest spirituality represented here. Or anywhere. The love of nature, of the trees, of the earth, of the waters. Wicca was what man glommed onto before man even had the words to identify god. It's the oldest religion known to man."

"Oh please!" Clara exclaims. Louder than you've ever heard her voice before. Emboldened by her wine. "That's completely debatable. Besides, all the teenage Goth girls who make up the majority of your 'religion'" —Clara purposefully air quotes the word— "don't know a thing about ancient ways. They learned everything they know about paganism from *Buffy the Vampire Slayer*."

"Besides," Muambwo chimes in, "life originated in Africa and the Yuroban culture was the first to identify the Orishas and worship them."

"Muambwo, your religion is so dependent upon Catholicism to even exist. You need all our candles and saints to—"

"That was simply a means of adaptation so as to avoid the unholy persecution of a people and a way of life. A persecution enacted by the holy men of your faith."

"Right. After their own leaders sold them out of the tribe and onto American-bound ships. That's a beautiful adherence to sanctity."

You. You are surprised at the flaring temper simmering beneath Muambwo's calming voice. At the sarcastic lilt to Matthew's.

What does not surprise you is Mark. Mark leaning back in his chair, smiling. Smirking. Mark and his jihadic melting pot.

Muambwo stands from the table, excusing himself from the conversation and heading toward the kitchen door. You follow him and grab another drink from the refrigerator, offering him one.

Mark calls from the living room. "All the food's clean. As is the beer."

Muambwo grabs the beer from your hand. "I'm too angry to eat now, anyway."

You leave him in the kitchen and rejoin the group in the living room. Ambyrr is but, but, butting her way unsuccessfully into the conversation while Clara insists the beginning of cognizance and thus the beginning of spiritual worship was with Adam and Eve, thereby solidifying Judaism as the oldest religion.

"I can agree with you there," Matthew admits. "It's just a shame you people failed to recognize the Savoir when He came to save your freaking souls."

"Amen!" Jude raises her hand to her tiny gold cross, clutching it tightly in affirmation.

"Jesus was not the only profit of the times."

"Oh shut it, towel head."

Matthew is on a roll. You. You think his god must be one hell of a powerful and vengeant being if he's willing to burn these kinds of bridges. Or the Vatican must really have some clout in the wet works business.

Haripreet sits to your left quietly, barely audible as he chants something to no doubt grant him with peace and serenity.

Mabel stands through the argument, thanking everyone for welcoming her home, and says she's ready to retire to her room. She gives you a wink as she passes by, whispering "you should be taking notes" before disappearing down the hallway.

Even through the raised voices, the faces of your guests look amiable. You study their eyes for anger and see only the glint of self-assured pretension. Of superiority. Superiority and slight amusement.

Muambwo returns from the kitchen with his empty beer bottle.

"You know," he yells, "I'm really appalled. I expect more from the likes of you. Disagree, sure, but at least have a modicum of respect."

"There are many similarities between each of our faiths," Alia offers. "We should not judge each other but be open to—"

"A bastardization of spirituality?"

Haripreet looks surprised the words managed their way through his vocal chords. His cheeks turn the color of your sun burnt scalp as he lowers his head suddenly.

"Come back as a cockroach!"

Jude. That was Jude. The sweet, blond treasurer of the protestant church. Jude clutching her cross. Her symbol of redemption from sin. Her emblem of servitude. You think it must be so easy to be pious with the Monopoly card of prayer at your disposal.

Mark leans over to you smiling. Smirking. Mark's grey eyes are wild. He whispers:

"See this? We made it through dinner peacefully enough, but every single one of them is frightened. They have doubts. They don't believe their god or God or gods can be tested and proven. Their anger is really fear. Fear that they are wrong. That they've dedicated their lives to something that was never there to begin with. It's almost delicious."

Mark's smile is mischievous. Like he had this planned. Like he pulled the trigger, added the catalyst to the Petri dish.

You. You shake your head, grab your beer, and head out to the back porch.

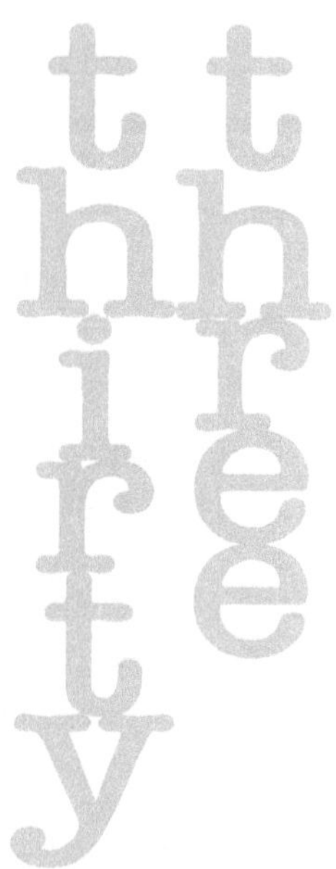

"Where do you think this is all supposed to end up?"

Huh?

"Why do you think you're here?"

I don't know what you're—

"You look like shit."

You become acutely aware of a dull ache crisscrossing your left cheek. You swallow hard and the pain sharpens in an overlapping pattern, pinching the skin above your chin, around your lips. Your mouth is dry and hollow. Even before you open your eyes you can feel your head spinning, grasping for something to cling to and finding only your stomach. It's almost a moment of clarity. Almost.

"I don't know what you're talking about."

Mabel smiles down at you as you squint in the vibrant morning sun. You lock on the same four teeth, the slightly yellowed canines that welcomed you home your first day in the house.

Mabel's nose tenses and snorts as she bends down to your face.

"You smell like aftershave, alcohol poisoning, and over-the-counter mascara."

"I'm not wearing any makeup."

Mabel. Mabel laughs. "You're not wearing any aftershave either."

"Leave him alone." Mark's voice is amused as he passes into your line of sight, carrying an armful of beer bottles. "He's hung over."

Mark's concern would almost be endearing if he hadn't let the screen door slam shut as he entered the kitchen. This is what you're thinking. These are your synapses finally firing.

You pull your head up and wipe the dried spit from your lips, from the seat of the folding chair you apparently spent the night glued to. Mabel looks freshly showered as she plops down in the chair. She rubs your head roughly while you peer around the stoop and into the backyard.

"Mark and I got most of the beer bottles back inside already," Mabel says, offering you a cigarette and lighter. She picks up one of the few stray bottles still lingering at her feet and props it beside your knees. "You can use this one for an ashtray."

You thank Mabel and take a few moments to inhale the smoke, letting your mouth begin to water and saliva sooth your throat. Inside you can hear the rattle of beer bottles and silverware, the remnants of last night's dinner party, as Mark tidies up the kitchen.

"I take it you haven't watched the videocassettes yet."

Your twisted mouth tells Mabel your answer.

"Did Mark find them?"

"No. I've got them all in the break room at The Morning Bean. I just haven't gotten the chance to watch them yet."

"You'll get to them. No pressure." Mabel leans down to drop her cigarette into the brown bottle beside you. She adjusts her black Lycra sports bra nonchalantly. "Have you been writing much?"

"Not really," you admit and brace yourself for a condescending glance. "I mean, not nearly as much as I should be. I think."

Mabel simply smiles as Mark appears in the doorway. He laughs. Mark's laugh.

"You should think about grabbing a shower," he says to you.

You nod and pull yourself slowly to your feet, fighting to stabilize your shaking knees. Mark holds the door open for you as you force your feet through the house.

Behind you, Mark and Mabel speak in a whisper. You. Omnipotent you. You know exactly what they're saying.

"Is he writing yet?"

"Not much. Just some notes. Nothing concrete."

"Looks like I was right all along."

You could have sworn Mabel had been the one questioning Mark's choice before. You. Omnipotent you. You clutch your throbbing head and turn the shower knob.

thirty four

"Hair of the dog?"

Mark offers you a beer as you rejoin your roommates on the back porch. Tiny beads of water cling to the short hairs that have just started showing on your scalp. You sigh deeply as you sit down on the top step and twist the cap from your bottle. The Saturday morning traffic on the 75/85 Connector is just starting to pick up as the city dwellers head to the suburbs for the water parks and shopping malls and the folks from outside the perimeter move in for a slice of city life. You wonder if the two groups even realize the passing. If the grass is simply greener because everyone they see if reveling in its difference, in its newness.

You. You can't help but smile as you lean your head back onto Mark's knee.

"Looks like you two have gotten close," Mabel smiles, shooting an I-told-you-so look in your direction.

You twist your mouth into a smile as you wait for Mark's response. Mark. Mark smirks. You feel his leg tense against your back, and you lean forward as he stretches his leg straight out, his foot dangling beside your face briefly before planting back on the porch. You. You pretend not to notice how he placed his legs down, just outside of a comfortable place for you to lean. You take a swig of your beer and gag, leaning forward to set it on the step.

Mabel laughs. "'Let the credulous and the vulgar continue to believe that all mental woes can be cured by a daily application of old Greek myths to their private parts.'"

"Oh, please. 'There are aphorisms that, like airplanes, stay up only while they are in motion,'" Mark laughs. "I can quote Nabokov too."

Mark seems happy to have Mabel home. You turn around to face the pair, taking note of their eyes glancing meaningfully at one another. There is a slight amount of white powder on Mabel's shoulders, smearing into the black Lycra sports bra covering her breasts. You smile as you picture her, in her room, trying on each of her many wigs before placing them atop the mannequin heads lining her bookshelves.

Mark. Mark looks exactly like he did the day you met him. Sitting there smiling. Smirking. Sitting there in a white t-shirt and black cargo shorts. His eyes locked on your sunburned and peeling scalp. Your head itches from the newly grown hair follicles forcing their way upward.

"So, what's on the plate today?" you ask, rubbing your scalp and wondering if Mark has scheduled surgery to re-grow your foreskin so Clara can circumcise you. You. You're only half joking.

Mark leans back in his chair and looks up at the sky. "Some mornings," he says, "some mornings you can almost see the blankets of exhaust swirling upwards. It makes you wonder if God is up there, choking for some fresh air. If the angels are all weeping into their Birkenstocks because they can't fucking breath."

"Don't tell me you're concerned for the environment," Mabel laughs.

"I thought you were an Atheist," you say.

"I'm just saying its probably a hell of a lot easier to breathe from beneath that smog-filled high horse. A hell of a lot easier to relax. And today is a day for relaxation. I think yesterday was busy enough. We can just hang out. Nurse our hangovers." Mark looks pointedly at you. "Write."

It's your turn to quote Nabokov. "'The pages are still blank, but there is a miraculous feeling of the words being there, written in invisible ink and clamoring—'"

Mark. Mark cuts you off with his laughter then looks at you sympathetically. "Come on," he says. "Where's your conviction? Who's right and who's wrong? Think about that and put it on the page."

"I don't think it's that simple. I mean, there has to be something to it. The massive similarities in religious beliefs from vastly different areas. All these individual peoples could not have all sensed the same thing without some sort of divine intervention."

"Just because they didn't have planes doesn't mean they didn't know how to walk. Besides, history is constantly being rewritten. Whisper a secret to little Molly Mayweather and by the time it gets to Charlie Tucker Molly's best friend wants to fuck him in the covered slide at recess." Mark smiles smugly. "Now all you have to do is rewrite history again. It's not that difficult."

"What about folk beliefs? Seven years' bad luck for breaking a mirror versus seven years of Hell for breaking a commandment. At least in an end-of-times sort of perspective."

"You don't think Old Wives read the Bible?"

"Or maybe the Antichrist is just going to be really fucking ugly. Or sing opera. Or both."

Mabel laughs at her comment. Or at you. You aren't really too sure which.

Mark. Mark says that if you simply think about it accurately, acutely; that if you understand that the Jews created monotheism as a means of empowering a people, of making them "Chosen" and denying the existence of a bevy of gods that came before. — *Too many gods to keep with with? All your crops and money going to sacrifice? Why not try the new and improved One?* — That if you realize that at that point history was reworked and centuries of civilizations since have adhered to that conclusion of setting, that exclusion of divinity, it is not a far leap for the next awakening to be that of atheistic origin. Mark says that if you consider the vast contradictions within the Bible, within the Koran, within the church and its nitpicky extraction of moments to correspond with whatever the hell it's trying to pass off as the law of the day; if you consider all of these anomalies it should be a fair path to a world of no gods.

"The court of law," Mark says, "is reliant upon reasonable doubt."

"Law is man-made."

"Exactly my point."

The sun is creeping past noon and beginning to blind you as you squint up at your roommates. Mark thinks you should be taking notes. The story is inside of you. Straight from his mouth.

"What about you, Mabel? What did you conclude? I mean, you did this once, right? With your video camera."

Mabel opens her mouth to speak but is immediately silenced by Mark.

"Mabel's movie is a different story." He is only slightly hiding the irritation in his voice. "You should focus on your own."

Mark. Mark rises from the chair and turns to the screen door. He glances over his shoulder and smirks. Mark's smirk. He says, "I told the folks at The Morning Bean you wouldn't be able to work there any more. Don't worry about your part in the bills. I've got you covered."

Mark lets the screen door slam, the crack harsh and brutal alongside the noises of flies and zooming automobiles from the highway.

Mabel takes a swig from her beer and stares out at the horizon.

thirty five

Write. That's why you are here. That's what you tell yourself. You force your eyes away from the white walls of your room. From the glow of the fluorescent bulb hanging naked in the center of the ceiling, bouncing and glaring off of the blinds. You stare at the off-white pages of your notebook, at the pale blue lines begging you for words, for glyphs, for symbols.

Groaning, you flip through your notebook to find the notes you took while speaking to Ambyrr, to Harry, to Alia. You find your description of Leonard's calloused hands, harsh and dirty, gently thumbing a twisted and burning joint in your direction. Of Muambwo's pectoral muscles. Of Clara's perfectly white teeth outlining her words with a chosen sense of precision.

Write.

The pen in your hand feels foreign. You. You wonder how you can tell a story you do not understand. If that is what creates intrigue. If that is what keeps you interested.

Your door swings open, and Mark strides in nonchalantly. He steps behind your desk chair and slides his hands over your shoulders.

Massaging. Gently. He bends down and puts his lips next to your ear, so close that they brush against you as he speaks. As he whispers.

"I'm sorry I was so cranky earlier," he says. He tells you he is just being irritable because he had a lot to drink last night as well. That he must be a little hung over also. That he just assumed you'd be happier if you had more time to write. That's why he quit your job. That he really only has your best interests in mind. He tells you this like a psychiatrist would speak to a schizophrenic. Slow and painful. As if his life, your life, depends on not pushing the wrong button, saying the wrong phrase. He says, "Why don't you close your notebook for a minute."

Mark. Mark moves to the edge of your bed, sitting and motioning for you to join him. He smirks and raises his eyebrows.

"I really should keep working. I think I'm on a roll."

You lie. You lie as if Mark doesn't know your pen has yet to scribble a word today.

Mark smiles and lays back on your sheets. He closes his eyes and whispers to the ceiling, "I just figured a nap would be nice."

You. You look from your notebook to his heaving chest. Quietly, you stand and join Mark on the bed, pulling convex into his body as he closes in around you.

Mabel. You swear you can hear Mabel laughing from the other room.

thirty six

"This shit is fucking gold! It's got motherfucking top ten bestseller potential written all over it!"

You sit in a hard chair, nervously picking at the green plastic seat. Pulling bits of semisynthetic polymer free and dropping them to the matted, forest green carpeting. The fabric is pulling free of the baseboards around the edge of the office. Hard water stains strain the carpet dye around clapboard bookshelves stacked and caving with bound books and loose manuscripts.

You stair at the slick greasy hair of the portly man spewing profanities from behind his desk. His hands fidget around the twenty-three pages of notes Mark typed up from your notebooks.

Mark. Mark smiles and winks at you from the plastic chair at your side.

"This Ambyrr character," Malcolm Young continues, "She's so damn hilarious. And Leonard..."

Malcolm goes on and on about the character studies from your notes. Your book. The beginnings of something great. Something definitive. Something holy. His body rolls around the seat of his chair as he speaks, as if each puff of air is realigning the molecules of fat, the chemical compounds of his body. Making the buttons of his pinstriped dress shirt arch and wrench against the force of his stomach. His chest. You. You pray the clip-on tie, the muddled red and blue expanse of cloth, will strategically fall into alignment to save your eye when a bombardment of buttons gives way. You. You pray.

Malcolm's office is in the far back corner of an industrial office building just outside the perimeter of the city. Tucked away on the thirteenth floor of the second in a series of three buildings making up the Walter Monroe Office Park and Suites a few blocks from the highway. Past a series of marble columns that haven't witnessed polish since the Office Park opened ten, fifteen years ago. Beyond the offices of the certified public accountants, the have-you-been-injured-in-an-accident lawyers, the distribution centers for local porn companies.

Malcolm. Malcolm is an agent Mark found in the phone book. A literary agent. The guy who's going to get your book in contact with the right publisher. The guy who's going to make all your dreams come true. Your dreams. Mark's dreams. Malcolm is that man. That man who will put every considerable ounce of his being into making you a star. Into getting out of his office park office and in the building with the big boys in New York. That's what Malcolm tells you.

Malcolm, who cannot complete a sentence without throwing in the word *fucking*, without *shit*. Without *twat*. Mark picks him because his ad is the largest on the page. In the phonebook. Mark picks him because he likes the font. He says it proves this Malcolm guy knows something about marketing. Mark drives you up to the parking deck, leads you through the building, traipsing along the matted carpeting. Mark brings you here because he thinks, Mark thinks, that he can convince you to write a little faster if there's an offer on the table. An agent who can hook you up with stardom.

Malcolm the agent, your agent, tells you the Marquis de Sade snuck his papers out of his holding cell, out of the insane asylum, through a nurse he seduced. That underground presses worked overtime despite a ruling from the French government banning all smut and pornography. Like the French could ever take a stance against indecency, he says. Malcolm says. He tells you how all those cocks and pussies, all that bondage and philosophy, all of it was tied up like a Japanese businessman waiting for a high heel to grind into his ball sac. How all of that life-altering shit was published in the face of all that controversy and all of the naysayers and all of the bannings and the book burnings and all of it became top market shit. Raking in the big bucks. Changing generations of fuckers. Literally. The literary agent says. Changing generations of housewives into sadists, into slaves, into Old Guard or New Guard. How the Germans ain't got nothing on the good ol' Marquis when it comes to fetish.

Malcolm, your agent, tells you all you need is three solid chapters to pitch to a publisher. He tells you this thing is going to catch on like wildfire. That it doesn't matter how small the first press is, people everywhere are going to want to get their hands on this.

"This ain't no shitter-read," Malcolm says. "You won't see no husbands propped up on the john turning the pages, no housewives using it to wipe down their twats. This is big business, boy. Book Club discussions. News stories."

You. You ask, "Don't you think it may be a little controversial? Mark told you on the phone what it's about right?"

Reinventing the Bible. Disproving God. Rewriting history.

"Controversy sells, kid. It fucking sells. You get a preacher condemning you—— Hell, get a fucking school teacher pushing to have it removed from the school library in Podunk, Utah, and the bookstores can't keep their shelves stocked.

"You guys came to the right place. Give me three chapters, boy, and I'll have publishers crawling up your ass and begging to suck your dick. You have my word.

"I'm so goddamn sure of it, I'm only gonna charge you a twenty-three percent commission instead of my usual thirty for first timers. That'd be licking my own asshole if I wasn't so sure this thing was going to produce the cash. Trust me, kid. I got it down on this end. You just give me the book."

thirty seven

The Presbyterian Church reminds you a lot of Jude's cross. Plain but elaborate. No sign of the torture of a young man in his thirties except in the "Praise Jesus"es sounding periodically from the Bible Study groups holed up in the various rooms along the corridor. They've got different assemblies for different age groups. Groups for married couples, groups for singles. The kids are divided by boy and girl. The older kids wield their *Teen Word of God* Bibles like shields, like swords. Like a status symbol. Relying on the Word to be retranslated yet again to fit into the hip-hop slang of the youth culture.

The inside of the main hall, the auditorium, seems like a disco nightclub as you pass through. West facing windows cast neon shades of red, of blue, of yellow into the aisle as you move. Behind the pulpit, a choir stands lazily, the three male basses at attention working on some hymn while the rest of the choir, the sopranos, the altos, the women with soul but no real key, they all slump in their seats until the choir director turns his attention toward them. Bits of gospel lead you through the multi-colored lights.

And the cleaning crew. Sniffing up dead leaves and shards of grass, butterscotch wrappers and loose change that didn't quite make it into the offering plate with ShopVacs. Blasts of air going for a lower tone than the guys on stage could hope to achieve. Deity Disco meets German Industrial.

And everything is plain. Solid colored cushions on dark oak pews. The pulpit more a podium. The cross behind the choir, old and rugged, held together with glue. Not a single nail visible. Even the stained glass windows seem plain. Like all the coloring was an afterthought. Painted onto the glass after the install. Black lines tinted that way instead of leaded into place. The result of the children's aisle at Hobby Lobby.

You pass the unused organ and push through the swinging door Mark told you would be there. The one leading behind the congregation hall into the bowels of the beast. You pass the short set of stairs leading up behind the choir. The stairs leading to the plexiglassed pool of tap water used to scare Jesus into the lives of babies with attempted drowning, then present them through a window to the pews and the choir and the hymnals. You reach the door marked "Treasurer" and tap lightly with your knuckles.

"It's unlocked!"

Jude sits behind a massive computer screen, aggressively typing figures into spreadsheets. A pencil lodged behind her ear, amidst her blond-white hair, meeting her red fingernails periodically to scrawl notes on the numerous spreadsheets and Post-it notes littering her cedar desk. Her thin red lips twist upward as you enter.

"I'm almost done," she says. "Give me one minute and then we can chat. Have a seat."

You plop down in the pluush green leather chair before her desk, running your fingers along the tarnished brass orbs hiding the chair's seams. Your eyes dart discretely over the spreadsheets, the totals of the monthly tithes versus the income of the congregation. The church always knows. The allocations for the cleaning crew, for the choir robes, for the pastor's new Beamer.

Jude notices your eyes.

"I'm trying to budget for the Christmas sermon. It's months away but the board of directors really wants us to bring in this guy who sang for the President last year. They think it'll bring in more bodies."

"The president of the church?"

"Of the United States."

You cast your eyes downward as Jude punches a few more numbers into her keyboard with adamant force.

"Done," she sighs. She sighs and says, "So welcome to our church."

Jude tells you she's really sorry about what happened at dinner the other night. The argument that erupted. She tells you she's not really sure what some of those other religions are about, but her church is about compassion.

"That's our motto," she says. She says, "'Compassion in Christ'."

Compassion is really what it's all about. Jude tells you this. She tells you that what separates her church and the protestant faith in general from the old ways — the ways of Clara and Alia, of Muambwo and Ambyrr — what separates her from them is that they live under the old laws. Laws that no longer apply. Laws of vengeance and serpents. Eyes for eyes. Hands for masturbation. Her church, she says, lives in the Age of Grace. The time encompassed by the love of Jesus. By His Mercy. His ultimate sacrifice.

"I didn't think he had a choice."

"He could have run away. He could have fought."

"The Roman Empire?"

"Yes. He knew what was coming and He chose to accept it. We all have choices," she says. "He chose to die so that others, centuries of others, may live a life in eternal glory. In heaven."

Sometimes, you think, *cowardice is simply staying put.*

Jude clutches the cross at her throat.

"Not to be rude," you say, "but if I were sent by my father to be persecuted and strung up on a cross, the last thing I'd want to see on the people praying to me is a constant reminder of the Roman torture device that did me in." You say, "Not to be rude."

Jude laughs. "The cross is a reminder of that sacrifice He made for us. For you. For me. It is a reminder that we all have crosses to bear. That we will persevere. Jesus carried his cross proudly. He submitted to the stones, the thorns. And He lives on."

You, too, can have your very own Zombie Jesus. Just add guilt and watch it rise in three days time.

"Speaking of crosses," Jude says. She shuffles through the papers on her desk. "I hope I'm not being too forward, but I couldn't help but notice the other night." She finds what she is looking for and slips a pamphlet across the mass of spreadsheets and into your hands.

You look down at the informational guide to *Angels, Not Alcohol: the First Presbyterian Support Group for Alcoholics and their Loved Ones.* At the smiling Christian faces finding family and friends and green collared Polos in the place of hops and barley. You give Jude props for hiring a recognizable catalogue model for the pamphlet cover.

"Don't be bashful. I've battled the demons of alcohol myself. In my younger days," she says. You look at Jude's young, twenty-six-year-old face, wondering if she took swords to banshees at twelve. "It's a really great program." Jude says, "I think we would really be able to help you."

thirty eight

"Myopic. That's the best word to describe those guys." Ambyrr is talking over her shoulder, plugging in Ethernet cables, tracing wires with her fingertips through jumbles of color-coded knots. "I mean, you'd think that Haripreet guy's whole way of thinking doesn't center around he and his people considering themselves better than the rest of us because they've been reincarnated as Hindu; because they've managed to be good enough to transcend."

Ambyrr, she says "transcend" with an added flourish of sarcasm. Like she knows she's the one who's really found the light. Like her name change proves that.

"And Clara and those Christian Mafia folk. How they're able to just ignore centuries of evolution and the Egyptians and the Greeks and the Romans and all of their gods who were real and tangible and turning into swans and fucking young maidens long before the Bible was ever dreamed up."

You. You've never seen Ambyrr so flushed with fury. You hide a smirk that Mark would be so proud of as you watch her hands pushing rapidly through wires and hear her tone rise and fall with the same galloping cadence she normally uses. Only this time it's littered with anger. Only this time it's hidden under the desk in her sunroom.

"Got it."

The computer on her desk pings as she rises to her feet and turns to you with a smile. All the animosity is gone from her face.

"Sorry for the technical error. Now I can show you what I spend all my days and a lot of really late nights working through."

What Ambyrr shows you is what she refers to as "An Online Cornucopia of Charms, Herbs, and Stars." That's her tagline. That's the phrase that rotates on a banner around a crescent moon at the top right corner of each page. That's what is on the banner pulled by the same freaking fairy that's tattooed sullenly on Ambyrr's back. Minus the mushroom.

"Are these spells?" you ask, fighting off the mental image of Ambyrr frolicking naked in the moonlight with the Great Hoofed One, discussing makeup tips with Beelzebub.

"Somewhat," she beams.

"All of them yours?"

"Goddess no!" she laughs. Ambyrr laughs with a bevy of exclamation points. "The site works like a wiki. That means its got user-generated content. Like those online networking sites that are all the rage right now. I've got close to two hundred thousand users, and each one of them posts their own Book of Shadows."

Ambyrr. She tells you a witch's Book of Shadows is kind of like a diary of sorts, containing all their magic, or at least the message of their magic. She tells you how words get passed down, but how there's no real set dialogue.

"'An' it harm none,'" she says, "'do as thy will.' That's the Wiccan Creed. That's the one rule we live by. Magic is just manipulation of the elements. Like science. Like chemistry. We witches have just figured out how to use nature, to worship the gods of nature in order to make things happen that are real and karmic and tangible."

Sort of like mind over matter.

"Oh, but it's so much more than that," Ambyrr chirps. "It's mind over matter and matter over mind and nature over everything. It's wholly consuming and wholly fantastic!"

Ambyrr says that everyone will have slight variations. That's why there are over twenty thousand spells and charms to find a lost loved one. That's why the site can continue to grow and flourish.

"And I just landed a huge advertising deal with one of the biggest online herbal suppliers! That's how I can afford to keep my sweet little witty kitties fed and in litter!"

Ambyrr drops to the floor and reaches her hands across the arched backs of the fourteen cats circling around her, taking turns in her lap.

"How'd you get the curser to be that little fairy with the trail of dust?" You ask. As if you're really interested.

"Oh, it's a simple CSS code actually. I thought it was a nice touch. Isn't she just the cutest?!?"

Ambyrr talks with a multitude of punctuation marks. You can hear the exclamation points pile onto one another. You smile a "she's beautiful" and take Ambyrr's urge to sit before the keyboard.

thirty nine

"What do you believe?"

Mark has never asked you that before.

Mark has never asked you that before, and you sit dumbfounded on the dark grey sofa, staring blankly into the empty fireplace.

Mabel sits Indian-style on the floor at your feet, gently combing through one of her Victorian-styled wigs, shedding droplets of powder onto the floor and rubbing them nonchalantly into the area rug.

"What do you believe?"

Mark repeats his question without a hint of urgency to his voice. He's beside you on the couch, staring ahead into the same sooted brick of the fireplace, not even bothering to make eye contact. As if your response doesn't really matter. As if he's just waiting for you to set him up for a tirade.

As if he already knows.

"Well," you offer, unsure of where to lead the conversation. "I guess I was raised Christian. I got sprinkled as a Methodist when I was an infant. And then went to the First United Methodist Church in my hometown for a few years with my parents. After they split, my dad switched over to the Baptist Church and I went there with him for a while. Neither of them goes to church at all anymore though."

And I go to every single kind of church you can dream up for me, you think. You think, but you don't say aloud.

"Figures," Mark says. Mark says, "You were raised in America. I mean, fuck. Here we got an entire country of fat bigots doing 'God's work' in wars, killing people over oil, and not even looking at the rights and privileges of its own citizens!" Mark starts up on the animated invective you'd been expecting. "Homeless people everywhere. Priests touching little boys. Prison systems holding men in temporary solitary confinement for over eight freaking years in Illinois. Clinics getting bombed and terrorists going free. And then claiming a separation of church and state. We can't rehabilitate because we can't bring god into it. Like we need god for rehabilitation."

"And gay people can't even get married. Where's the separation of church and state in that?" Mabel chimes in, almost laughing, almost winking at you.

"It's because all the pundits, all the congressmen and the lawmakers and the right-wing zealots, they're all claiming it has nothing to do with the people and everything to do with the Bible," Mark again. "Which is not supposed to be a part of it. And the freaking left-wing nuts are just as bad with swinging that pendulum so far around it tetherballs back to knock the shit out of everyone in the wake. What the hell is wrong with socialism? With everyone in this nation being given the same rights as everyone else? Isn't that a hell of a lot closer to god's work?

"This country got its start with people fleeing Europe to avoid religious persecution. With people wanting that freedom. They even wrote it down on parchment like Luke or John etching out a chapter. And here we are, flinging witch hunts and oil drills around like freedom is only applicable if you get in fucking line with some seventy-year-old fucker's concepts of light and dark."

Sometimes you wonder if Mark ever really has to breathe.

"But you still didn't answer my question," Mark says, and repeats it a third time. This time he turns to you, smiling, smirking. Sitting there on a calm edge like he expects you to say something profound.

You want to say how you believe in what you can feel. But then you think of Ambyrr and how she thinks you can feel god tangibly in the trees, in the soil. And how Clara and Matthew can feel God in their guilt. And how Haripreet feels god in his trances.

"I believe in Mark," Mabel laughs from her perch on the floor.

"Thanks, Mabel. That's really helpful."

forty

Pierre Bourdieu once said something about words like "sorcery" and "magic" being used to disqualify religion and the term "religion" being used to qualify your own brand of sorcery. Not yours, exactly. But one's. Anyone's.

Of course, this is someone who also felt the need to *say* that "the most successful ideological effects are those which have no need for words." Your guess is either Bourdieu had a really stellar sense of irony or was a little too self-absorbed. Like those people who rudely tell other riders on the public transit system they're being rude.

The other riders. Not themselves.

Looking around this bus, no one is quite that self-reflexive. That's what you're thinking anyway. No one, not even you who's spending so much time considering them, considering Mark, considering what Mark and his entourage of mystics have to say.

Mark woke you up this morning with a poke to the ribs and twenty singles for the bus. He told you your itinerary like a flight attendant directing you to the nearest exit door in case of emergency. Urging you to plug your nose and just jump. If the parachute does not inflate, oxygen may still be flowing.

Mark has filled up your day with lectures. You've got a ten thirty with Clara and an eleven forty-five with Haripreet. You're meeting Harry for lunch since he's no longer fasting and you're meeting Alia after lunch. You're rounding out your day with a visit to Matthew and a priest or two who will be there just to wonder what it'd be like to grab your ass.

Not really on the priest part. You just think it could make the day seem a bit more interesting.

Mark, he gives you twenty singles for the bus which should be just enough as long as you don't make any pit stops or get on the wrong bus or off at the wrong street. Hopefully Harry will cover lunch.

What you're supposed to be doing, what you're supposed to be thinking is already all tied up in your mind, aching in your pen, spurting out of Mark's mouth.

Your half hour with Clara is supposed to make you think about origins. You're supposed to consider which came first, the chicken or KFC. Mark. He wants you to talk to Clara and figure out how a religion is formed and how it progresses and what happens to those who refuse to change with the times. He wants you to understand how a big bunch of dentists can embrace x-ray technology and have a hard time getting on board with a new prophecy handed down by their god. How a group can play god with Tay Sachs testing instead of playing God's vengeful will and let His nature take its course.

Haripreet is there to preen, to talk to you about a religion of evolution. He's intended to make you wonder what happens when technology is embraced and adorned with incense and garlands. He's there to make you see that not everyone's afraid of dying, as long as they're going to get reborn. He's there so that twinge of doubt at the rebirth of things glimmers behind his iris and gives you another chapter to focus on.

Alia is there to show you another trinity within God. That Christian, Jewish and Muslim faiths all worship the same top dog. To make you see that progression within is not always going to be progression beyond. To show you that she'll still have to don her head wrap and pretend she doesn't have trouble seeing while she's driving.

Matthew is there to give you hope. And, according to Mark, a comical side to your work. Because if you can't find the irony in Paul —in a devout atheist who starts the first church— where can you get your chuckles?

You. You choose to find your laughs within the chaotic comfort of the parading progression of spiritual ambiguity Mark subjects you to on a daily basis. You try to ensure your chuckles don't sound like cackles as you cut off eyes beaming with holy light, as you interrupt lips expounding the many virtues of the many gods they uphold in order to make your next appointment.

You. You try to suppress a sigh as you drop your bag inside the doorway and stumble toward your bedroom. It takes all you've got to hold back a booming guffaw as you push open your door, step into the stark whiteness you've come to call home, and almost trip over the chair to your desk. The chair that holds eighteen tiny videocassettes. Mabel's cassettes. Sitting there, propped up in your desk chair in three stacks of six. Propped up there like the copy of the porno mag you stole from your father's nightstand and your mother found dangling with the ripped shards of lining protecting the base of your box spring. That copy of *Club International* your mom swears dropped from under your bed while she was cleaning, sweeping, vacuuming. The porno she sat on your desk chair and waited for you to get home from school and see and come clean about. Fake tits and airbrushed abs. Fake sex photographed, attributed to false names, and left sitting in your bedroom. Taunting and teasing.

Three stacks of six. Eighteen.

And not a VCR in sight.

You have to pretend to explore the candy bar selection when customers come in. You have to debate the flavors and possible combinations thereof for the slushee machine. Not because he's embarrassed by what he's telling you. What he's saying. No, it's because what he's saying, what Leonard says he's telling you, is the real deal. It's serious shit that would blow the minds of those lesser fucks coming in to buy stale Doritos and gossip mags, six packs of PBR and pizza pockets, it would blow their minds straight out through their ears, dripping grey matter like they'd just gotten hit with a gush of electrical current.

Leonard would know.

What Leonard says is that the QuickSave itself is a micro-macro-cosm of the nation as a whole. Those aren't exactly Leonard's words. You, omnipotent you, you're paraphrasing.

Leonard says that you could hang out there for an hour, that all you'd need was an hour, and you could boil the future of our country down to teenagers and disc jockeys, beer and cheap condoms.

And Mark. Mark is doing his part for the future generations of squealing pre-pubescent jerk-offs with a safety pin and a stack of Trojans.

Leonard tosses a pack of cigarettes onto the counter with a pile of coins before turning to you staring at the rotating hot dogs, greying at the edges, wrinkling and puckering on their spits. The teenage representative of our future grabs the smokes and pennies, thanking Leonard a little too profusely. Leonard. He doesn't even turn.

"Get the fuck outta here before I check your ID."

You keep your eyes on the spinning, processed pork; your fingers picking at the burnt red crust around the edge of the ketchup pump as the doorbell chimes, signifying the customer's exit.

"Take that kid," Leonard says. Leonard says, "That kid is the future of America. Soiling up his lungs with tar and cyanide and whatever else the FDA is trying to experiment on those citizens it deems as lesser for dropping their cash on a confederate cash crop, slowly trying to kill themselves to escape their nine to fives and the evening news reports. He's what we all got to look forward to."

Leonard says, "Let's grab a smoke."

Outside the Quicksave, Leonard lights up and takes a deep drag. You stumble along beside him as he rounds the gas pumps, picking up empty soda cans, tossing credit card receipts into the trash bins they barely missed as drivers sauntered back into their vehicles. The cherry of his cigarette goes from red to orange to grey as it dangles and bounces from his lip. Leonard. He's wiping down the signs saying you must be sixteen to pump gas. The signs telling you the shit is extremely flammable. Leonard. He's talking and ashes are falling to the ground, blowing into the pools of Technicolored oil spills left behind by beaten up old Cadillacs with spinning silver rims and red and gold crown air fresheners stuck to the dash in their rear window.

"I had this one guy at the GDCS—"

"The Georgia Diagnostic and Classification State Prison," Mark chimes. You didn't even know Mark had come outside with you. But Mark, he's leaning back against the padlocked cooler with five pound bags of ice for a dollar forty-nine. He's leaning back with a cigarette hanging from his lip and his leg propped up against the "C" in "ICE," leaning like James Dean, ready for his car crash.

"I had this one guy on the Row. He was studying for his GED. He'd sent off for one of those study-at-home guides where you answer a coupla questions about five apples going into a basket and Isaac Newton's head coming out and mail it back and get a certificate sent back to you so you can hang it over your cot so you have something to stare at while your cellmate's fucking your asshole raw. The other guys on the block used to rib him constantly, not violently but verbally, they used to fuck with him about how he wasn't gonna need no general equivalency where he was going. He was about to get as generally equivalized as a person could get.

"But that fucker, he was a better hope for our cunt of a country than any of these fuckers stopping in here for antifreeze and ice cube trays. At least he wanted to learn. At least he cared about going out with the knowledge that he had a piece of fucking paper printed up to look like parchment that said he'd finished the equivalent of what a Georgia high school kid is supposed to finish. And he was gonna go out still knowing it instead of dropping it all with a weekend drinking binge and a fraternity pledge.

"He's the only one still gives me chills to watch cashin' in. Watching his eyes all brimming with that knowledge before that canvas drops over his head. That's some fucked up shit, man."

Leonard is done smoking, finished meandering about the pumps. He's walking back into the store with you in tow. With Mark still leaning up against the cooler, lighting another cigarette.

"You still watch the executions? Were they televised?"

"Some of 'em. They was all recorded though. But that televised shit, that's for pussies. I got the real deal. Not just what was on the evening news, but the whole thing. The live, unedited-for-live TV cuts. You'd be surprised what they can clip out in that five second delay. I paid off one of the tech guys at the local station to grab me copies of all the ones I worked. At first I just wanted some gory shit to show my buddies, to offer up as conversation at church gatherings or dinner parties. But after a while, I started watching to see if I could tell who got to kill the fucker. Or who *had* to kill the fucker. It became all about guilt; checking to see whose wire was the live one. If Jimmie pulled his lever just a half second before I did and that shock went buzzin' just a half second later, I could know it was me who burnt the shithead up.

"I never could really tell though.

"But I got a tape for every single one of those offings up in a box in the attic. Every single goddamn one."

You think for a moment about the images captured on those tapes. About the ghosts that could haunt them. You think about Mabel's tapes.

"You don't happen to have a VCR, do you?"

Leonard, he looks at you for a moment, considering.

"You sick fuck," he finally says. "Looking to get your rocks off on some real death?"

"I— uh, I wasn't," you stutter.

"I'm just fucking with ya, kid."

You sigh, give a faint laugh. Your eyes tilt to Mark still propped up outside, checking his watch, tossing his cigarette toward the pumps.

Leonard, he smiles. He says, "Who the fuck has a VCR anymore?"

Mark says you'll get your fill of rum and chicken's blood at the party. He says spirits will be high — contagious even. Mark. Mark tries to crack a pun. Either that or he's trying to scare you off from possible possession. Mark says that because the event will be so rich, you, the three of you, should take the subway. Because being drunk on public transit beats the ditch off the 85.

Across from you an old black man sits creating his own universe. Becoming his own god. His balding head is ringed with grey, and the harsh light in the train reflects on his scalp. His right arm swings out in fierce motions. He grabs for invisible foes, catching them in a deft outreach and slamming them against his knee before another thrust of his hand discards their limp and lifeless bodies. His hand swifts downward as if gathering root vegetables by their greens and extracting them. He little-bunny-foo-foos them hard, tosses them aside and stamps demandingly on the floor. Asking for more or to cover up the hole left by his conquest, you aren't too sure.

Mark. Mark nudges your shoulder and looks at you conspiratorially. Still, he doesn't lower his voice as he says, "So where do you think god is in all of this? Is this part of god's perfect image? A man so fucking ape shit he's slaying imaginary demons on the southbound train?"

The man looks at you with pity in his eyes. He looks at you like he pities you and scratches his crotch before thrusting his arm out again to catch whatever ghost is hovering at the corner of his eyeline.

Mabel laughs as you pull into the next train station. She stands, mimicking the old man's movements as you beeline from the subway car and make your way out to catch the bus.

forty three

As soon as Mark exits the bus, he pulls a bottle of Malibu rum from his bag. Mark. Standing there, blocking the people exiting the bus, blocking the people trying to get on. Mark breaks the seal on the cap and takes a long, hard swig. He holds the bottle toward you.

"I thought that was supposed to be a present for Muambwo," Mabel says.

"It is," Mark acknowledges, capping the bottle and dropping it back into his bag.

Furious public transit riders, those riders who were already furious anyway, are huffing and puffing as they sidestep Mark. Mark, still standing there. Mark lighting a cigarette. The bus driver is giving her best evil eye to the back of his head. You can tell she wants to say something. But years of getting screamed at by riders, getting honked at by taxi cabs, getting flicked off by kids in their shiny new SUVs; years of all that have humbled her. Instead she just sighs, waits for the last passenger to enter and drop their fare, and closes the door.

Mark hears the rumble of the engine starting off and begins walking down the street, you and Mabel in tow.

"So, he gets a new name again tonight, huh?" you ask. You ask as if you didn't know this, as if Mark hadn't been chastising the idea of a godly name change for the past week.

A man in a Grateful Dead t-shirt and a pair of baggy, bleached blue jeans coughs as he passes the three of you, moving in the opposite direction, making a spectacle of his forced seizure of the lungs, keeping it going as he stops walking completely.

"Excuse me, sir."

The three of you keep walking. You wonder how much conditioning it took to get you to ignore people on the street. How many times people begged you for change before you caught on and kept your eyes trained on the horizon.

"Sir!" The man calls again. "Could you listen to me?"

He breaks down coughing again, exuding a bevy of forced groans, going for that phlegmy retch but coming out sounding hollow as Mark spins around and moves well within the guy's personal space. But he doesn't speak. Mark doesn't.

"I'm allergic to cigarette smoke. I'd really appreciate it if you put that out."

Mark looks down at his cigarette, staring into the red cherry as if considering his options. You. You can see them flash across Mark's face. Through his grey eyes. Put it out; continue smoking; or put it out on the poor bastard's forehead, against his temple, in his left iris. Mark inhales sharply on the butt, exhaling a long stream of grey into the man's face.

"I'm allergic to shitty cologne and aging hippies. If you hadn't stopped me, that's all the less of each other's vices either of us would have been forced to inhale."

You wonder if Muambwo will be any different under whatever new name he's taken. If, when the Romans decided they needed to go for a younger look, Jesus was really any different than God.

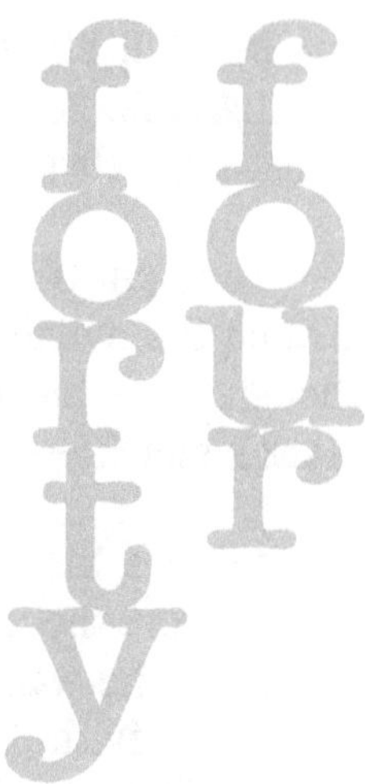

You expect people to be dressed up in silk and satin; wrapped in beading and sequins; bright colors; wielding knives. To look like African tribesmen bred with Mexican wrestlers. Like a matador mixed with a pop star. A Saturday Morning Cartoon's ethnic diversity wet dream.

Instead, they're all dressed in white. Like a bitchy woman at her stepdaughter's wedding, forgetting the virginity of the bride. Muambwo doesn't seem to mind though. There're no nails digging into bouquets, no sideways glances and shoulder pats from bridesmaids. Instead he's all smiles as he greets you, the three of you, at the door with a brown paper bag. He tosses the bag at Mabel with a wink.

"I figured you would insist on wearing black. Please put this on. You can even pull it on over what you're wearing now."

Mabel smirks and rolls her eyes before pulling the light grey fabric from the bag. She pops the elastic waistband in her hands before following Muambwo's directions to the bathroom.

Except they aren't Muambwo's directions.

You can tell already just by looking at him, at his small dreadlocks, his smiling eyes, you can tell already that this man is no longer searching for something. He's no longer Muambwo.

"I am Obadimeji," he proclaims, watching your mouth try to wrap around the syllables. "In ritual. Obadimeji is my praise name. You guys though," — he looks at Mark and smiles a smile that almost mimics Mark's smirk — "you guys can call me Justin."

Mark clears his throat and asks where to drop off the booze, if there's a keg out on the back porch or an ice luge in the kitchen. He wants Obadimeji, he wants Justin to fill you in on the ceremonial aspects, on his newfound faith in gods before the drinking starts, before the others arrive. He wants you to take notes.

"Do you get to pick your own name?" you ask. You ask with your notebook open, pen in hand. Like a half-bit reporter sniffing out the scoop. Like you're back in high school working on an editorial for the Mid-State Eagle.

"Yes and no. The name is given by the orisas. But it's based on me, on my path. On how I interact with the divine, with myself, with the world. So in that sense, it is like choosing my own name. Though I didn't find it in a book of baby names and point it out."

"He wasn't asking for a jaunty walk down Philosophy Lane," Mabel is behind you now, baggy grey sweats hanging sloppily over her tight black Lycra. "Just say you didn't pick the goddamn name and let it be."

"Mabel is just upset her tits aren't popping out of the sweatshirt I'm making her wear."

"Oh, right, Olillammaringadingdong. I'm the one who's upset." Mabel pulls the relaxed cotton fabric tight around her bust and, with a fake pouting huff, heaves it into Justin's face. "I'm so upset I need to drink my tears away. Point me to the booze."

Justin smiles and nods toward the kitchen.

"Is that where the alcohol sans chicken blood and crazy island herbs like Rohypnol is kept?" Mabel raises her eyebrow wickedly before heading through the doorway to join Mark.

"I know Mabel's attire can be a bit— well, alluring. But what's with the sweats?" you ask, trying desperately to make sense out of your surroundings, out of the familiarity Mabel seems to have with the house.

"It is improper to wear black in front of the orisas. Mabel's been to the ilé before. She knows better," Justin smiles. He smiles and says, "Look, as long as they're both in the kitchen, why don't I just give you a crash course on what's going on.

"The house, our place of worship, is called an ilé. Of course, it's not our only place of worship, as devotion remains with us at all times, regardless of faith. Or at least it should. Tonight's event is basically a big birthday party. There are shrines set up for the orisas who guide me. All the blood offerings have already been completed. No chickens running around with their heads chopped off tonight."

Justin smiles at your pen rushing across the page of your notebook. He's trying to make you laugh. To make you understand the joy of the occasion.

"My name," he continues, "means 'king who was crowned twice.' Which is an aspect of Shango, the god of lightning and thunder. The god of maleness. As in intense masculinity."

You. You could swear that smirk on his face is one of seduction. You could swear it is identical to Mark's.

"I think it was divined as a joking jab at me," he says. "Seeing as how I've been migrating through so many paths in my life.

"The orisas do have a great sense of humor. Or maybe I just think everyone and everything is funny after a year with no fucking."

You remember what Mark had told you about Muambwo's, Justin's, Obadimeji's iyagwo period. You remember their sly glances. Muambwo changing his white tee shirt after slaughtering the white hen.

"I'm so freaking glad that year is over," he smiles.

forty five

The rum burns as it hits your gullet. Even though it's for the gods, years of economic hardship have evolved the offering culture of the ilé toward the largest handle of the cheapest liquor available. You don't really mind though. It works, and it's free. Besides, you think, maybe Matthew would be able to take the lesson back to his church.

"Our work is grand because our faith is grand," Matthew says. Matthew says this well within earshot of Justin. Judgment, even as he's here to support and celebrate Justin's spiritual coming-of-age.

As if she herself were affronted as well, Clara pipes in, "We believe our body is a temple and therefore we are careful about what kind of swill we put into it." She bares her white picket teeth as she raises the bottle of natural spring water she carried in herself earlier in the evening.

Your head instinctively twists toward Ambyrr, sure that she will have some sort of input. But she is several steps away, visibly forcing her hand to remain a few inches away from the shrine to Obadimeji's Shango.

You suck down another swig of your rum and Coke as you remember Mabel's welcome home dinner, avoiding Jude's eyes as her mouth twitches in a tally of your alcohol intake. She should only be on two, but you're certain she's added at least five more to account for the time prior to her arrival.

Everyone from the dinner party, everyone of your informers is here. Everyone except for Alia. As liberal and forward in her religion as she and her father may be, a pagan co-ed late night festival of blood and alcohol is still a little much to ask. You wonder if Mark realized the limited interactions you would be allowed with Alia, if that in itself was part of the lesson. If he simply figures today's political climate has marginalized the Muslim faith enough already in all but a few bleeding hearts so its importance to your story is, in turn, able to be minimized.

The others in the house, the other practitioners alongside Obadimeji, his new family, his godparents and god –sisters and –brothers, they are all welcoming but standoffish. They don't make it obvious though. No, they're all moving and laughing, chatting and mingling about with the revelry of welcoming a new recruit. Dancing in such a way as to make sure Justin believes he's gotten his money's worth.

You join Ambyrr next to the shrine and offer your glass in a toast. She barely glances your way as she clinks her cup to yours, her eyes fixed in their constant movement among the items laid out in bowls and soup tureens, sitting among sequined cloth or covered by satin.

"A part of me loves the folky, vaudeville aspects of all of this," she says, never taking her eyes away from the bright colors set out before the two of you like the set of a new children's show. You fight back mental incarnations of pedophiles in furry costumes with memories of Ambyrr's own alter, more subdued in its earthy evocations, but just as gawdy with its fairy effigies.

"It looks like Broadway blew chunks all over Barnum and Bailey."

You didn't hear Mark join you, but you can't help but laugh at his comment. Ambyrr's eyes flick toward the two of you momentarily, and the candles highlight her frizzy brown hair with all the humidity of Cuba.

"This is a sacred place," she warns. She warns as if that would mean a thing to Mark.

"And the holy has no room for carousing."

You turn to see Mabel standing behind you, offering you another glass despite Jude's disapproving gaze. Mabel. She's tied up her sweatshirt in the back, pulled it taut across her breasts and knotted it high enough to expose her stomach. She's rolled down the top of the sweatpants Justin gave her to several inches below her navel.

As Jude and Haripreet join your group by the shrine, Matthew wanders the house, taking note of how closely the seven-day candles mimic the Catholic iconography of his own candles, and Clara flags down a party-goer in search of a recycling bin for her water bottle.

"That's not at all what I mean," Ambyrr insists. "The gods, anyone's gods, are nothing if not a place for joy and good tidings." Your eyes scan over Jude and her pamphlets; catch on Harry and his sovereignty. "What I mean is, this altar, this holy shrine is a gateway and should not be mocked. Even if these gods are picky about whom they let into the fold."

"I don't know about that," Mark stirs the pot, beckoning toward the red, black, and cheetah print offering plate that has slowly filled with cash throughout the party. "It would seem to me that if enough money were thrown their way, these guys would have no problem welcoming anyone into their sanctity."

"Like a high class hooker," Mabel offers.

"Or a mob boss. Ten to fifteen grand for an initiation is like mob money."

Mark and Mabel lock eyes in amusement while you watch the gears visibly turn in your companions' heads.

"Do you not spend your money on wigs, Mabel? Or you, Mark, on your books? Or Matthew and Jude on their tithing?" Haripreet asks, his voice calm, his third eye dilated. "The problem here is not with the cost. It is not a purchasing of faith. The real issue lies within the assimilation of false deities."

You look from face to face at the smug fortitude that appears, aware that even in their agreement, each person in your conversation is trying to one-up the others; that everyone here sees their god as the one who is not false.

"Be they false or not," Ambyrr says, "what kind of faith system imports that some do not belong?"

Ambyrr one-ups through openness.

"Not all are ready for the divine." Haripreet. You think of his caste systems, of preparing oneself for the death of a thousand deaths of ascension.

Haripreet one-ups through birthright.

"But the one true God is always ready for us."

Jude one-ups through elitism.

And Mark. Mark one-ups through silence. He one-ups through a striking gaze in your direction: an unspoken prompt to speak.

You. You gather your strength from fermented molasses, from the sweat of the men in Barbados gathering sugarcane.

"I would propose," you propose and take another sip. "I would propose that this — this shrine, this party, this collection of various peoples — that all of this is a perfect example of bringing the notions of the one true god concept into question.

"Look at Matthew." As if on cue, as if he's been waiting for his name to be called, Matthew starts across the room to where you are all standing. "He's been busying himself noting the similarities between his and Justin's faith. Or at least in the representations present in both.

"From my understanding, Lucumi is an assimilation of the traditional African Yuruba faith and Catholocism. People adapt their practices all the time. To fit in with the modern. For survival. Judaism becomes Christianity becomes Modern Day Saints." You take another gulp of your rum as Mark smiles and nods in your direction, egging you on with his approval. "I mean, what does this do but tell us that your gods —all of your gods— could be interchangeable?"

You almost expect Mark to applaud as Mabel reaches out and clutches his arm. Instead, Matthew speaks from your side.

"This amalgamation of faith is not one sanctioned by God. It is of false prophets. Of the Satan's bastardization. Turning God into a polytheistic faith is simply bringing idols into play."

"What of your Mary? Of your Saints? Of your Christ or your Holy Spirit?" You turn quickly at Clara's voice, wondering when she wandered over. "Are they not idols placed before your God?"

"Actually," Justin chimes in, walking calmly over to join your discussion, "my faith is a monotheistic religion. There is but one god, one creator — as is true even in Haripreet or Ambyrr's polytheistic devotion. The others are merely aspects, saints or angels if you will, to guide and interact with the world."

"I just know I wouldn't want to live like that," Jude says, crossing her arms across her chest, making sure her tiny golden cross is still visible. "Without the light of God in my life. As a non-believer."

Your eyes shift rapidly over the faces of your companions as Mark opens his mouth to impart his own wisdom. Mark. Mark says, "I wouldn't want to live with a slack jaw and a colostomy bag, but Stephen Hawking seems to get along just fine."

You. You're trying to figure out why this accumulation of people drives you to the sauce. You're trying to understand what it is that shifts the energy of the room. If it's the brutal attempts at keeping your stories straight. Mark's stories. Mark's lies about your interests. If it's the collective's unquestioned reasoning in assembling.

You only see what you're wanting to see.

You. You're trying to figure out where the hell Mark got off to. Where Justin is.

"Wake up."

It comes as a whisper, seeping in between the throbbing of drums on rum labels, quietly trying to coax you to your feet. To your pen.

"Wake up."

It comes in the gentlest form you've ever heard Mark's voice take. It's enough to frighten your eyes open, this change in character, in humor.

Mark. Mark is propped up on his elbow beside you, his hand tracing your cheekbone gently, his eyes gleaming with the reflection of sunlight fighting its way through your tightly sealed blinds. You can feel your head begin to emerge from the swill of ocean currents, from torrents of dreams, as bird songs filter through to calm you.

"I got you a new notebook," Mark says. Mark says, "I really think it's time for you to write."

Mark is on his feet. He's checking the number of notebooks on your desk. Making sure the pens work in circular motions. Mark is inching toward your bedroom door. He is grabbing the alarm clock from your desk and mumbling something about watching time as avoidance. He is telling you to get cracking. That it's for your own good. That it's time to get it all out. Onto the page.

Mark. He is telling you that he's doing this for your own good. He's telling you he'll be back at lunchtime.

As your eyes clear, you notice a bagel and a glass of orange juice on your desk, next to the notebooks. As your ears clear, you hear the click of a key turning, of a deadbolt sliding into place.

You. You think, *Very funny, Mark.* You think, *what if I've got to piss.* You think, *I may as well get started.*

On your desk is your stack of half-filled notebooks. Of quickly jotted descriptors and observations. Church pamphlets and the little green bag filled with herbs and cat nail clippings Ambyrr gave you to help you write better.

You have yet to fill up a notebook. You have a tendency to start new ones on a whim. As if by starting fresh you'll have a renewed interest, a muse, a motivation.

Not that you aren't interested. You just have no idea where to begin.

And today doesn't feel any different.

You sigh and pick up a pen.

forty seven

Mark is relying on his atheism to prevail, to enter into you, into your story. He shows you faith — its similarities and its differences; its hypocrisies. He thinks you'll see the similarities for their hegemony, their utter ridiculousness. He thinks you'll see their differences as proof of disproval; you'll see their hypocrisies as a lack of the divine.

It's brilliant, really. Group them, these religions, all together and you can strike them down in one fell swoop. Disclose their differences and you suddenly find a displayed diversity incongruous with a single truth. Disproving the single disproves the all in turn. And being a hypocrite, well, that just allows for a swift and easy write-off.

Everything is laid out, wrapped up, ready for you to unfold onto the page. The story, the one that's inside of you already. The one Mark wants you to tell.

What Mark isn't counting on, though, is you, is your mind. You pushing it a step further. You including him, his atheistic nature, in your discussion. Or maybe he was. You. You're realizing figuring out Mark's thought patterns is impossible, is moot.

Still, you recognize his atheism for its zealotry; his passion as thick as that of those in praise.

If one it so disprove god, god in all forms, you think, *does the nature of the human condition insist upon the placement of a new religious almighty? Like a ruling hierarchy? A monarchial heritage?*

Atheism as a means of becoming god.

You try to imagine Mark with a *tilaka*, with a pentacle, with a cross.

In your studies, Mark takes you to devotees, to meetings, to churches, to his father. He takes you to the park to ingest mushrooms on wheat toast, smothered in peanut butter and honey to quell the bitterness of the natural hallucinogen. To ask god to appear. To stare at the man in the ill-fitting suit, sweating with the humidity, broadcasting epitaphs for a lost power through his portable PA. The street preacher ogling the park for sinners and the misguided.

Before the mushrooms work their way into your cranium through your digestive system, before they've worked their natural magic on your optic nerve, as you're laying out your checkered blanket, setting up your picnic of bottled water and sandwiches, you focus your gaze on the man's coal-colored skin. His eyes shift over you just as quickly as yours do him. He peers to Mark and to Mabel and on to the others skipping work for a Tuesday afternoon outing to the park. His pupils are as large as you feel yours becoming, the whites of his eyes appearing jaundiced, yellowed further in their bulging relation to his dark, ebony skin.

His tongue is too large for his mouth, but he's managed to conquer the lisp. He talks with his hand, the alternating one, the one not holding the microphone, to divert attention from the mound of dark pink flesh fighting his lower mandible, his puffy bottom lip. You wonder if this held him back in seminary school, if that's how he ended up here. You wonder if he went to school at all – if it is even necessary for understanding an innate god.

"Maybe he thought he could reach those most in need on the streets," Mabel offers.

"Yeah. And get a quick hit or a blunt fuck behind the benches when he takes a break," Mark says smugly, sinking down to lie on his back and stare up at the sky.

You take a seat next to Mark, crossing your legs Indian-style, in the lotus position, suddenly wondering if that classic phrase was referring to Buddha or Geronimo, taking the bread Mabel is pushing in your direction. You eat quickly, the honey, airy and sticky on your tongue, doing little to force the earthy grate of the fungus into a palpable taste.

"For we are all sinners in the eyes of the Lord. Your rollerblades are an affront to the Almighty. He sees your sodomy, your greed, your gluttony." The street preacher has a message for everyone who passes. He speaks to no one in particular. "Repent now and the Kingdom of Heaven shall be yours! When God comes for you, and Lordy He's gonna come, He will know you and He will know your sins and He will forgive you if you take Him into your heart."

This is where your memory cuts off, where the rest of the day becomes a blur. You blame the drugs circulating through your system, but Mark, Mark likens it to the prophetic experience. He speaks of trances and near-death traumas. He talks of the blinding majesty of gods. How the memory is jarred, is divided. Glimpses. Moments. How any man who decides to write it all down later has no option but to get half of it wrong.

You can't look at the monster and write about it. You have to look away and experience it in your mind alone.

"There's bound to be error," Mark argues.

"So are you granting the existence of a divine entity?" you ask, feeling playful. This is before Mark plays at locking you in your room, before you sit, pen in hand, starting to realize how much you need to urinate and how locked the door is.

"Not in the least," Mark replies. Mark replies casually and tosses a small bit of gravel toward the man still ranting to his PA microphone.

Mabel giggles as she peers up at the sky. She rolls over to her side and focuses her gaze between you and Mark, not really looking at either of you, but not exactly looking away either. Mabel, she says, "We all know that the grass is green and the sky is blue."

You and Mark nod your heads. Somewhere inside you are aware that were it not for the substance percolating through your system, Mabel's stoner-logic would deserve serious ridicule.

"What I'm saying is," Mabel says. "What I'm saying is, we all know it's blue or green because we say it's blue or green and then we all agree on that. But what if my blue and our blue are different things? What if your blue is my green and my green is your blue?"

You lie back on the grass, catching glimpses of blades out of the corners of your eyes as you look toward the robin blue space above.

"I think god is like that," Mabel says.

Mark expects you to find the light, to find god, in all of these moments. He expects a twisting catharsis, churning slowly in its immediacy.

Mark expects you to find the lack, to find the chaos, in all of these moments. He expects a bubbling doubt, springing silently in its obviousness.

He expects these things from you, when he's locked you in your room, when he's supplied you with notebooks, when you've really got to micturate.

Your pen scratches against the paper slowly as you attempt to capture the paradoxical state of your story, of your situation. Your bladder aches and your concentration shatters as you cross and uncross your legs uncontrollably.

You feel a presence before you hear the shift of the lock. You are quick on your feet as your bedroom door begins to open, sidestepping Mark and slipping into the bathroom, slamming the door quickly. Locking yourself in. You almost laugh at your feet, mocking the elementary school-styled pee-pee dance while fighting with the button on your jeans. As you begin to feel relief, you perk your ears toward the door, listening for Mark to cajole you. Or to apologize. Neither comes.

You flush the toilet and barely glance into the mirror as you wash your hands. When you emerge from the bathroom, you find Mark in your bedroom, leaning against your desk, shuffling through your papers.

"You've made some progress this morning," he smiles, though his expression is telling you your progress is not nearly enough.

"It's really hard to concentrate when you've got to piss," you reply, invoking all of the smugness you see in Mark's eyes. "That really wasn't funny at all."

Mark is silent, considering. Although you're almost certain he's in no way considering you, your anger.

"Mabel can move into the living room for a couple of months," he finally decides, making the statement like it answers all your questions. "I can get a door up to the hallway this afternoon. That way you'll have complete access to the pisser whenever you need it."

"Why would you need to install a door?" you ask, incredulously, after noticing no change in Mark's serious demeanor.

"I wasn't joking about this isolation thing. I think it's good for your writing, for finding your voice. It cuts down on the distractions. Forces you into your own head."

You think about your own headspace, about how much Mark would rather have you in his head. You think about the seriousness in his voice.

"Think about it," he says. "With this solitude, with this opportunity to write completely unhindered by any outside distraction, I'm giving you the chance to dwell not within the hustle and idiotic bustle of the minutiae of the inane existence of the everyday. Here, in this room, you can just be within yourself, within your story. You can really linger in and dissect your past alongside these past months.

"Henry James 'delighted in the past.' William Faulkner promised that the 'past has not ended.' They, both men, dead, but their words linger on. Derrida, now dead too, conversed with his own ghost in *Cindres*; his words of fifteen years prior being nothing more than the words of a ghost.

"These words, living on, become the only solid and yet ephemeral notions of these men. The words become the men."

You think of religious texts, written or passed down by firelight.

“That can become you. That will become you,” Mark smiles. He smiles to encourage you. To make sure you don’t feel like you’re trapped. To make sure you don’t feel like a pet locked in a carrier cage until its owner returns to toss you a bone.

“So I’m stuck here, trapped in my bedroom, until I finish this book?” you ask, allowing it to sink in, to sound as idiotic aloud as it does in your head.

“Oh, cheer up,” Mark smiles. He smirks as he brings his head closer, as his lips meet yours.

You let your eyes close with his kiss, taking in the taste of stale cigarettes, of coffee and whatever he ate for breakfast.

“I brought you some lunch,” he nods toward the sandwich and chips sitting on your desk. “And I got you a new radio.” You notice the small black box tossed onto your unmade bed. “Just to prove I do care about you.”

You. You can’t help but smile. You bite your lip to taste Mark again.

“It’s a small sacrifice, really.” He kisses you again. “Think about what I’m sacrificing in not getting to see you.”

forty eight

Your radio is your only window to the outside world. It gives you glimpses. Glimpses it would seem Mark wants you to hear. Fighting in Gaza. In Israel. Last night two synagogues in the Midwestern United States were vandalized by men, by kids, by children armed with spray paint and derogatory slurs. An Albanian family, cleared by the TSA, is still not allowed on their flight.

Mark could not have planned it better himself. The tension. The want to disprove. Not yours. Not your want. The want of the proverbial they. Of everyone else with a shred of self-conceived power to disprove another's faith. They — that proverbial they — they think they're proving their own by disproving another. They refuse to see the similarities. And even when they acknowledge them, the differences are too great. *He spells "god" differently. She's an idolater. He broke the First Commandment. His pronunciation proves he placed another before my judgmental, pompous, glory-hound of a lord. Father. Yahweh. Savior. Blessed Child. Jesus. Holy Spirit. God.*

You. You write in attempts to block out the dreams. You write names with asterisks beside them like you're writing a memoir, an editorial, a letter to Penthouse Forum. The story is true. Your version of truth. The names, dates, and major events have been changed to protect the innocent.

And you. You're the only one who can no longer make that claim. Innocence. Knowledge denies innocence. It suffers it. You. You suffer.

You feel yourself becoming feral. Which is a misuse of the word. Which is what you're fighting against.

You. You're caged; confined. The opposite of wild. And still there is a hunger slinking into your eye. You can feel it. Clawing and scratching and howling at the new moon of your pupil. Dilating. Widening.

Mark would call it your story — the Wolf-Boy crouching in your cornea. He would say that that wildness is the collection of words begging to be set free. To force pen to paper. You could counter that your words, your story cannot be devoid of human connection, of compassion and response.

You could counter with a snarling mouth at his jugular.

But you've not seen Mark since he took away your light — literally. He took away your light bulbs and left you with wax columns, with matchsticks to rub together.

Besides, you think. You think Mark would probably like that.

And as much as you picture your car parked on the street outside to remind yourself that you aren't really restrained in this house, shackled to this desk; as much as you picture grabbing the keys from their hook beside the front door and hopping in and flooring it; as much as you imagine all of that, you find yourself imagining Mark's lips. Mark's smirk. You find yourself rationalizing the good behind the motives. You tell yourself that this really is the best way for you to finish your work. Probably. Nose to the grindstone. As much as it may hurt.

Besides, you think. You think Mark has probably taken your keys from their hook anyway.

Letters look like violence when they're littered on the page. Sprawled out, crawling around begging to make words. To make a sound. Trying hard to form a voice.

Derrida talks about the *polylogue*. He invents a word your pen has no problem with, but spell check underlines in red. He's talking about voices. Your voice: you, as the writer and as the character. And the voice of the reader. He's talking about playing god. Becoming God. Inventing people. Creating them out of rambling black lines and clay and ribs. Encircling them and embedding them. Encasing them within a new mythology that has no choice to be anything other than true.

As if truth were that black and white.

As if truth is what you are striving for. What Mark says you're producing.

You. You hold a candle up — literally, not figuratively — to the battery-powered analog clock Mabel left outside your door a few days ago. This is what you're doing. Not what your words are trying to do. You hold a candle up because Mark, Mark in his infinite wisdom, Mark has decided that all the best works in history were written under candle light. That perhaps cutting down the buzz from the overhead fluorescent, cutting off the glare bouncing from the stark white walls of your bedroom, perhaps then you'll be able to concentrate more.

Now you understand why the room, your room, the room Mark had prepared for you, now you understand why it is so white. The candlelight against the paint glows. Illuminates. Highlights your notebook, your stack of notebooks. Makes the words okay. Makes them fight.

You've got the fire, now you're just waiting for the brimstone.

You imagine yourself as Jonah inside the belly of a whale. Making hand puppets on the wall. Making a choice. But then, that makes Mark God. And that's the last thing Mark wants. Or maybe it's the first.

Your dreams are haunting you with a catatonic abandon that's begging to get to second base but settling for a little over-the-shirt action. Your dreams, even when you're awake they're attempting to demystify your words, to empower them with dancing hamsters and kneading cats, elephant people with screaming daisies and clouded faces and snowy white beards and that little "Draw Me!" turtle from the match books and the five-cent-art-school applications.

The last time you saw Mark was five days ago. Five days ago when he was standing precociously upon the back of your desk chair, unscrewing the fluorescent light bulb and tossing you a white plastic lighter. One of those deals with a bikini-clad blond on the side everyone in your high school picked up on Spring Break trips to Panama City Beach. One of those that looks like the bikini was painted on and if you hold it tight enough, apply enough heat to the plastic, the bikini disappears and you're left with perky painted nipples and public hair that doesn't match the bleach job up top.

As you light candles, Mark tells you Leonard just got them in at his store. That he, Leonard, picked that one up for his son and actually got you one of those pens with the bare-chested Chippendales dancer with his black bowtie and bulging black thong that drops off when you turn the pen upside down. Mark, he pulls the pen out of his pocket and demonstrates the act for you in the growing light as you burn your thumb moving the lighter from wick to wick. Mark, he tells you Leonard got the pen for you, but he's going to hold onto it because it may end up being more of a distraction than an aide.

He says something about thoughts counting and leaves your room with a whirlwind of greeting card philosophy and your light bulb in his hand.

fifty

When you're writing everything down, you find it harder to compete with the barrage of details your pen spurs forth. The motions in your mind seem so much less precise, so much less surgical than even the haphazard melee you're writing. Your pen is giving them a cutting precision even as all of the pieces seem jarred and out of place. Even as the narrative is still coming together, cycling through the boredom of too much interaction followed by way too little.

At night you dream Mark into existence, feel his breath on your shoulder blades as he curves behind you, snaking your body. Spooning. His hand traces slowly down your arm, and you throw out one of those reflex smiles, debating between real joy and the joy-you're-supposed-to-be-feeling.

Two hands find yours in the darkness and you feel your body convex, arcing out to find the edge of the mattress with your gut, your head and feet angling for a central position on the bed, arms stretching out behind you in a king-of-the-world stance. Freefalling without a parachute. And Mark, all the time behind you, warming your neck with his rhythmic expulsion of carbon dioxide.

A sharp pain burns into your palms, into the arch of your feet, dulling quickly as the rush of warm blood gives way to a throbbing that is working to slow your quickening pulse.

Harsh in the dull light of your room, your bed falls slowly away and Mark's face moves into focus above you, the soft black stubble along his jaw line twisting with his sneer, his grey eyes almost glowing, they're twinkling so hard; almost matching the soft luminescence of the dim light on your stark white walls. His hands above your head seem enormous, clutching a brown crosshatch of wood. He twists the cross up on one end and your left arm raises, pulled up but still limp at the wrist, waving frantically as Mark's hand flicks above you. Another jerk of his hand and your foot raises, followed by the other, and you find yourself walking, marching, crusading.

Mark the puppeteer. And you, the marionette still bleeding around the nylon string punctured through your hands and feet.

Mark. Mark is smiling at your stigmata.

Laughing alone is a lot like drinking alone. It's a sign of trouble ahead. A red-sky-in-the-morning sort of situation. Not that you can see the morning sky. Not that you can get much more than a thermos of coffee and bottled water. But you. You find yourself laughing a lot.

It tends to happen when you first open your eyes. When you realize you were dreaming. When that doubt about the dreaming creeps in. When you're Rosemary wondering if your husband just violently raped you or if somehow a hoofed beast scratched the hell out of your back.

You laugh while pulling on pants. You laugh to tone your abs. You laugh and you pick up your pen.

Today your coffee is loaded up with turbinado sugar, brown and grainy, barely dissolved in the hot water filtered through ground beans and paper; held between solid and liquid by thick, refrigerated cow's milk. Or today it's more likely liquidized bean curd from the taste of it.

You let it gather on your tongue before it hits the back of your mouth with a sweet bitterness and your throat muscles contract in rhythm to aid the downward slope of gravity. That's what swallowing is, broken down into a still broad overview of its parts. That's what Mark wants you to do. Break it down into its parts but still keep it broad.

Mark. You're sure he was smiling, smirking when he dropped off the thermos and a bright red apple. You're sure he watched you wrapped up in your bed sheets, twisting and crucified on your mattress, a crown of sweat on your brow. You imagine Mark placing the apple down carefully and slithering out. But Mark. Mark is not a serpent.

You pick up the apple and break the flesh, sucking as the fruit juice dribbles down your chin. The skin of the apple is smooth in contrast to the crisp complexity of the meat, tart and bitter on your tongue. Everything tastes bitter now. Salty and bitter. Smooth and bitter. Bitter and bitter. You are fascinated by how tastes you never noticed play out in your sensory isolation.

Where your apple had been, perched atop the sprawling notebooks spread across the side of your desk that's not good for writing, that surface area above the row of drawers that hold more notebooks, that once held your mother's things and before that your grandmother's, you find a tiny slip of paper, folded and tucked away as an offering from outside the whiteness of your bedroom. A gift from Mabel.

Scrawled in her tight penmanship, long and taut with serifs arcing into the ascendant and descendant spaces are the words:

By their fruits, you will know them.

Matthew 7:16

Taken out of context like every preacher picks and chooses from the Bible for his sermons. A not so subtle play on words. On what you have written. What you will write. A warning from God filtered through Matthew and then Mabel.

They say — those Old Wives, those proverbial wise men and wise women and wise others — that the Devil always speaks truth to propagate his lies. That that's the power of his trickery. You decide then that the truth must therefore be trickery.

You. You wonder if that makes God's words lies. If by proxy of a dichotomic system, the opposite of true would be false. In an imposed macrosystem based on this or that, on Good or Evil; in an imposed microsystem based on black or white with no area for grey set between the two firm-lined notions; in a world like that, it would have to be true.

The Devil's work.

But what of non-dichotomic systems? What of Ambyrr's belief that good and evil are one, are held within each god? With the Wiccan's "do what thy will" giving a free range of access? Yet it is preceded by a demand to harm none. Still a judgment call on right and wrong. Good and evil. Still a binary.

Still, the truth as bad.

Mark. Mark's sweet eyes, his smirking smile. Mark's lips parting to release a barrage of blanket statements battled by a bitter bashing. You, the two of you, standing in the checkout line at the Goodwill. Mark telling the clerk her saccharine packet smile is marred immensely by the chew stains on her teeth and cannot be saved by her cheek jowls covering it slightly at the edges. Mark telling the truth. The truth hurts.

An' it harm none...

The truth is the Devil's trickery.

Trapped.

Becoming less than human. What is the writer? The practitioner? The zealot?

"We need a car."

Mark's voice is matter of fact, not at all harried. Not at all like what you're feeling. Still Mark is moving swiftly, the clacking hard soles of his shiny black shoes promising a swift break into a run as the pack behind you closes in.

"Yeah," you agree, increasing your pace to move in stride with your roommate. "These shoes aren't exactly made for escaping a mob of angry villagers."

Behind you, you can feel the horde edging closer. You. You think you can smell kerosene and matches as torches light up. You think you can smell the manure stuck to rusted pitchforks. You have the urge to duck from the possible onslaught of molotov cocktails.

You round a corner and leap over a toy poodle as Mark quickly sidesteps the sleepy woman letting her dog shit on the sidewalk once more before she goes to bed. The woman hears the coming crowd too, and quickly gathers the dog into her arms before rushing into her apartment building.

Mark grasps your collar, pulling you into the alley-styled walkway lined with dumpsters and blue recycling bins from the program the city decided was more expensive than the environmental impact. You lean against the aging brick wall with your hands on your knees, arching your back in a moment of temporary reprieve. You open your mouth to speak and Mark silences you with a stern glare.

In the shadows of the alleyway, tucked out of sight from the pouring gaze of the streetlights, you let your eyes adjust, your pupils dilate.

The tuxes Mark picked out for the two of you are sleek and narrow. Vests versus cummerbunds. Pinstriped. And though both are mostly black with soft thin bands of white, in the dimness of the alley, you can tell your stripes are centered directly opposite Mark's.

Details.

Your eyes follow Mark's to the mouth of the alleyway as a gaggle of sharply dressed men and women rush past. The men, too, are decked out in formal wear, though nowhere near as suave as you and Mark. The women, sequined and red, glinting like mating fireflies in the lamplight.

You hear the rustle of a flint against metal and turn to the sparking flame as Mark ignites the Lucky Strike perched on his lips. He gives you a wink as you deny his offer to join him in a smoke, still trying to catch your breath. He begins angling toward the main street and you join his gait.

"Why are they chasing us anyway?" you ask, realizing for the first time you have no idea where you had been or why you were there.

"Why does anyone ever get pursued?"

This is not the time for Mark's proverbial life lessons.

"I know," he says. Mark says and smirks at you as you find your bearings on the sidewalk, craning your neck to try to make out the street sign on the corner. "But even a night at the opera can hold a lot of truths you need to learn."

The opera?

Your eyebrows raise, and you peer over Mark's shoulder at the trim, short man moving closer at a rapid pace, his cufflinks flashing as his arms swing at halftime with his legs.

"They're back here!"

You spin on your heels at the short guy's words, taking in the well-dressed throng behind him pushing into a U-turn and closing in on you much faster than you would have imagined.

Mark. Mark tips his head to the short guy who's slowed to a brisk walk as he moves within five feet from where you're standing. Mark takes your hand unexpectedly and drags you out into the street, acrobatting around the oncoming traffic before quickening his pace.

"We need a car," he says again, still calm and collected. "Follow me."

The two of you push down a side street, leaping over the Oak and Magnolia roots jarring and cracking the sidewalk. You listen to the growing rumble of panting and clacking high heels navigating the path behind you.

"They're heading to the park!"

You blink suddenly as you see that they're right. The houses beside you look familiar now as you move down the street toward the open pasture tucked into the center of Midtown. You wonder what Mark could have in mind as he leads you into the inline skaters and behind-the-tree blowjobs abounding in the after-dark park hours.

You quicken your stride, more comfortable in your step now that you have realized your familiarity with your surroundings. As you near the edge of the park, you set your eyes on the downward sloping bike path before feeling Mark's grasp on your wrist tugging you away from the opening. He slows to a walk and places a hand on your chest, urging you to bring balance to your breathing.

There are more people on the street now, and you notice a line of traffic slowing as sharply dressed valets exchange car keys for numbered cards and smiling men escort their dates toward a dinner that will no doubt buy them a quick lay for dessert.

Mark signals for you to stop, his left cheek tensing as he heads toward the entrance of the restaurant. Two of the attendants drive off to safely park the vehicles of new money patrons already grown too lazy to fight for the limited city parking available. The third is busy angling himself away from the thin glass doorway so, if the manager happens by, the burning cigarette resting between his middle and index fingers won't turn into a pink slip.

Mark motions for you to move to the rear of the restaurant where the valets are pulling the vehicles into neatly packed rows. You turn to move, perking your ears toward the growing sound of footsteps closing in behind you as your eyes catch Mark's hand reaching into the cabinet of unwatched keys.

A few moments pass before Mark joins you, smiling at the keychain dangling from his fingers. He spins the chain twice before catching it in his palm and moving further into the parking lot.

"So your plan is to try the key in every lock out here until we find a match?"

You. You have no idea why that is what bothers you; why the notion of purloining a pile of pressed aluminum and pistons doesn't feel at all out of place.

Mark aims the key at the lines of cars, pressing the unlock-from-a-distance-because-a-twist-of-the-wrist-is-too-much-work button and waits.

No response.

The two of you push closer, moving toward the center of the tiny lot, Mark aiming and pressing. You try to denote an air of belonging, of being casual for the people jogging along the sidewalk bordering the lot. As swiftly as you may be walking, you are supposed to be here.

The rumbling of cracking heels and voices grows louder from behind you as the angry villagers sidestep into the parking lot to spot you among the vehicles. A horn honks twice in rapid succession, and you peer at Mark's smiling grey eyes as he beelines toward the driver's seat of a red Trans-Am with black tinted windows and a GR8GOD vanity plate. Laughing, you round toward the passenger seat, glancing at the affronted looks of your pursuers. But you aren't laughing at your sudden means of a get-away so much as the irony of Mark behind the wheel of this license plate.

Gunning the engine, Mark spins the car toward the exit. The throng of well-dressed men and women lock arms in a game of red-rover; a human versus human automation chicken match.

"So what's the plan?" you ask, bracing yourself against the dashboard to combat the sudden acceleration as Mark's eyes flick through the crowd gathering at the exit, accessing the situation.

"They're stealing a car!" one of the men shouts. He is tall with wavy brown hair, thick. His office-worker body strains against the seams of his navy blue suit.

"Your fingerprints are all over this car," Mark says calmly, and you peer at his gloved hands clutching the wheel.

When did Mark get gloves?

"I think god is mad at you. I said that with a capital 'g,' but you'll never write it that way."

You turn to the voice from the backseat to find Mabel riding bitch, her legs spread over the center console, a powdered wig in her lap. She looks comfortable in the villain archetype, alternating between stroking and brushing the headpiece in her lap as if enough Marsha Brady-ing could cajole it into a purring vibration.

"Why would god be mad at me?"

Mark is still allowing the engine to idle, revving it occasionally as he stares straight forward, evaluating weak spots in the linked arms blocking the exit. He barely turns as the three valets and what must be the restaurant manager bound around the building with clenched fists and wide-eyed fear.

Mark lifts his foot from the brake pedal, letting the vehicle lurch forward gradually before stalling to a rocking stop as his foot slams back down. He is testing the veracity of the gathering crowd, seeing just how far they're willing to go for their cause. Measuring in centimeters the minutiae of their instinctual backtrack.

"What do you think we should do?"

You know Mark is asking for Mabel's opinion rather than yours.

"If you're complacent for long enough," she replies, "any crowd will disperse." Her hand never stops working through the strands of synthetic hair. "His fingerprints are all over this car."

"The way I see it," Mark says. Mark says with the eerie calmness he's spent the evening embodying, "The way I see it, you've got the mob or the cops." He says this like he's giving you the choice.

You hesitate for a moment then begin wiping fervently at the dash with the sleeve of your tux jacket.

"That's a rental," Mabel says. Mabel says, "Gun it, Moses."

The Trans-Am lurches forward, and the gathered crowd parts as you pass through and out onto the street.

Mark catches your eyes in the rearview mirror. From their squint, you can tell that he's smirking. You hear a soft click of metal shifting and feel Mabel's arm reached between you and the door.

"There's always got to be a sacrifice," Mark says as the wind picks up and the door swings open. Mark's hand clutches your shoulder, and you feel it tense as his arm stretches taut. Ducking into a roll, you brace yourself for the rough and tumble of the asphalt.

You awake with your knees and palms on fire. You feel constrained and fight against the cords pinochioing you from slightly above and to the left. Surrender sets in, and you feel the muted warmth the southern U.S. summer takes on when it creeps indoors. The only sound in your room is the purr from your heaving chest.

Finally you allow your eyes to open, your surroundings hazy as your skull throbs and spins. The sterile whiteness of a hospital overwhelms you, but it lacks that antiseptic aroma of attempting to cover up death.

You. You're beginning to realize things. The spinning has slowed to a gentle ebb and flow, bobbing only slightly back and forth as your vision plays at centering. You fight the urge to laugh and vomit as you find yourself on the floor of your bedroom, your sheets twisted and roping around your naked body.

You were dreaming.

Your breath halts for a moment, as if your lungs need a firmer grasp on the air you're taking in. As if you need something to prove that this is your new reality.

You let your eyes adjust to the timid light bouncing off the stark white walls of your room — those walls that even in the darkness glow a pale grey, the grey of Mark's eyes. If you would have paid any attention in your high school psychology course you may be able to Freud up the lingering moments of your subconscious moving picture with some longing for Mother, life as the "other" psychobabble. As it stands now, though, now you are only able to grope around for a lighter, hit up the wicks to the tapered candles set up around your room like a cast-off set from a B-movie about almost-gay jocks at an all-boys school who shack up with Lucifer in a play to pass history, find you pen, and get to work.

You. You have to wonder what would happen if you just told Mark you finally understood what Nietzsche meant. If you say, after much consideration, that you agree wholeheartedly with Gabriel Vahanian, William Hamilton, and Paul Van Buren. If you offer up notions of theothanatology and call the hours spent locked away in your little corner of Mark's universe moot. You wonder if Mark would buy it. If he would agree that all of these thinkers agreeing upon the death of God, be it metaphorical or not, would cancel out your wager and let you throw down your cards.

Even without him here, even without the upward curve of his lips visible, without his grey eyes piercing into you, you can hear Mark's answer. Mark. Mark doesn't want you to kill off god. Mark wants you to assure yourself, assure the world that those loving arms of Heaven, of Utopia, of Nirvana, that those days of harps and Birkenstocks never were and never will be. Mark. He does not mean the message to be depressing. He does not mean for it to inspire fear. He simply means it as encouragement. To live. To be.

Mark. He sees your tome, your words, your story, he sees it as a means of escaping a lie.

You. You wonder if you have any means of escape yourself. If there is a way to slip out the window unnoticed. If you could lie in wait for your daily delivery of bread and water, pounce on the guard, and make it to the nearest payphone. If maybe you could tunnel your way to freedom.

If you really want to be set free.

Or if, maybe, you're just wanting to see Mark.

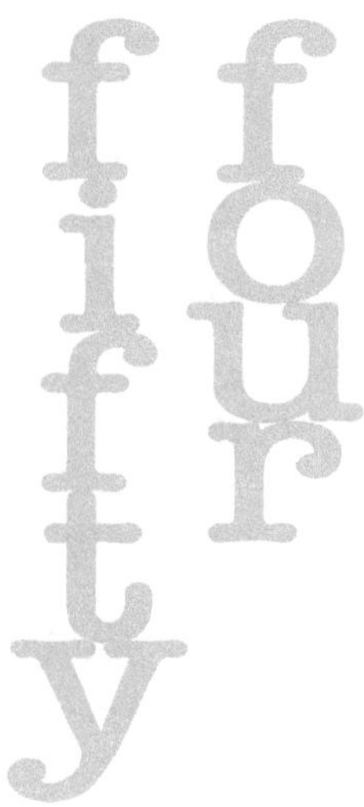

Glimpses of red. The gleaming glint of a knife.

You. You can barely make out the shapes as you enter the living room. You can barely make out the shapes despite wiping the sleep from your eyes. Despite the glowing embers — red and orange — leaping into yellow green flames in the fireplace. Leaping into the hottest fire. A moment of warmth in the cold, dark room.

But you can make out the malice. Or what you perceive as malice. Creeping into all of the faces you can't quite see. You know Mark is there. Is here. You can feel him. You can feel him as clearly as you felt him in your bed. In his underwear dying your hair. The knife in his hand sparks in the light of the fire.

"Sometimes." Mark says "sometimes" as if it's the most important word he's ever uttered. "Sometimes the best writing is written in blood."

You can see Matthew. You think of the crucifixion.

You can see Ambyrr. You think of the Crusades.

"Sometimes," Mark says. "Sometimes the blood is what makes the words flow."

You can see Clara. You think of the holocaust.

You can see Justin. You think of animals given to gods.

You can see Alia. You think of red staining the streets. Of that being everyday.

And then there's Mark. And then there's you.

You know you love Mark. You can feel it. Creeping through you. Out onto the page. You know you cannot escape it. Nature wants to conserve energy. Two pendulums will eventually sync in time. Something about neurology and brain patterns. Synapses firing. Mob mentalities. You know that if Mark knows you love him, he will love you too. You know you will write what Mark wants you to write.

Mark moves closer in the darkness. Mabel is flanked to his left. Her porcelain skin looks ghostly in the dark chill of the room. Haripreet. Jude. Leonard. The rest of them. The move around, spilling out of Mark. Circling you.

"Form a circle."

You stretch out the radius. Arms wide. Keeping your eyes locked on Mark. Feet together. Crucified.

And whosoever believeth in Mark.

All around you light from the fire erupts on blades. Mark's knife. Mabel's. Ambyrr's athame. Leonard's fish-boner. And you, in your underwear, straining to make out expression.

You. You feel fear.

Mark steps forward as the circle closes in. You. The two of you. Central and confined.

"Blood is what makes a martyr. Makes a hero. Makes a god."

"I don't want to be a god."

Your voice is strained and shaky. Hollow. It sounds from nowhere. You feel no air passing your vocal chords. Your held breath remains in your lungs.

"Not many people have a choice."

Mark's knife is at your throat. Pressing. You can't swallow. Your laryngeal prominence — your Adam's Apple — would jump. Would slice so easily.

Mabel's breasts press against your back. Her lips brush your ear.

"Think of all the people you'll save."

You wonder if that's what Judas told Jesus. If that's what the kamikaze bombers with their suitcases and pregnant bellies are told. If you'll get a bevy of virgins and all the mead you can drink.

You can make out Mark's eyes now. His smirk. Stretching across his face. Comforting. The knife traces down your chest, from your throat to your gut. Resting just below your navel. Outstretched horizontally.

Mark. Mark's smile. His smirk moving in. His lips meeting yours.

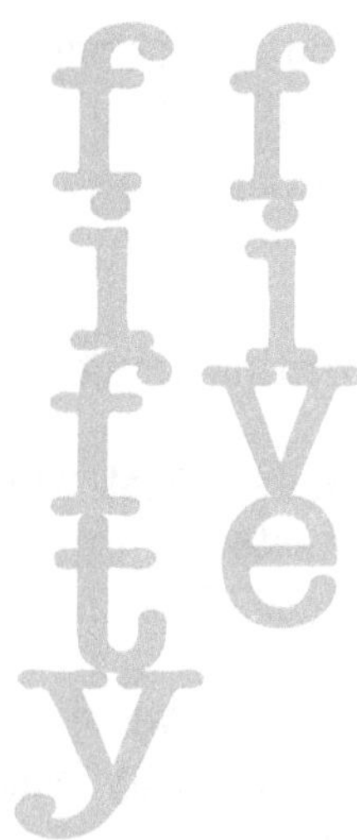

Monsters materialize in dreams.

In 1799, Francisco Goya etched *El Sueño de la Razon Produce Monstruos. The Sleep of Reason Produces Monsters.* He presented a world where men turned from rational thought and monsters were born. Where men adhered to superstition —to religion — and devils surrounded them.

Mary Shelley, tasked with the impetus to write, dreamed up Victor and his monster.

Monsters materialize in dreams.

Rabbi Loew, alone in his quarters, asleep in his learned state of glory, of holiness only God could give, received a message from the Lord. He constructed man from clay. Carrying out God's work in Eden. Carrying out God's word. Making Golem. Making monster. Making a monster that required a tablet, a word etched in stone, to move, to exist, to be. The Word of God to survive the day. The Word of God created Monster.

Writing brought it to life.

You awake with your stomach churning. Dancing. Jumping. Fighting hard to avoid the knife Mark dug into your gut.

Your eyes adjust in the darkness, trained on the ceiling. Darting to the door Mark installed for the hallway. The deadbolt locked, tight.

Writing brought it to life.

Write. That what Mark wants of you. To write to erase the monsters created by god. The priests pouncing on little boys. The holy men spilling blood. The anger and the violence and the vengeful rage.

So you write until your hand hurts. Until your pen spurts ink so haphazardly entire words are lost. Until your pen spurts ink so erratically entire thoughts are missing. Are merely scratched into your notebook. Traces.

God created everything.

So much so that you can see the trace of his being, of her light in everything on Earth. So much so that every abnormality — all those sixth toes and third nipples, snake-headed cats and platypuses — they're all warnings that the all mighty god is pissed as fuck. God creates monsters. From the Latin *monere.* A warning. An omen.

God's trace makes monstrosities. Your trace.

Your trace could undo it all. Could rationalize the monsters into Santa Claus.

Jacques Derrida does not believe in monsters. Or at least that's what you assume. He does believe in ghosts. Or at the very least his ghost does.

He wrote that each writing produces one. A ghost. A specter of the author at that particular moment. A haunting. Derrida. He had a conversation on paper with himself — on paper — from fifteen years prior. He chatted with his ghost about typographical errors, missed meanings, voices. *Polylogues. Cinders.* He creates a circle. Ever expanding. A Big Bang.

The writer becomes creator. Not just of words, but of specters. Of haunts. The writer becomes god. Without the writer would there be monsters? Would there be god?

Mark haunts you. Mark is haunting you. Both are active. But one feels so much more immediate. Pressing. Pressing like the knife in your dream against your navel.

You. You don't want to be a god.

And still you write. You write to avoid thinking about the dream. About what it could mean.

About prophets. About ghosts. Specters.

You write because Mark wants you to write.

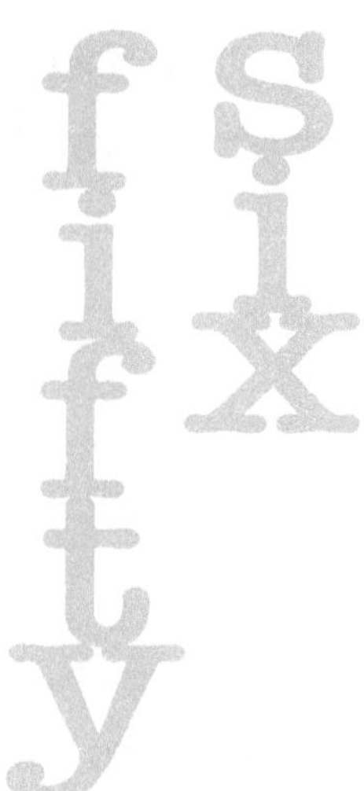

The story is inside of you already. Waiting. Waiting for you to conjure it up like magic. Like god.

That's what Mark says. He says it is complete. Like a divine, prophetic vision. The lion inside the cub. The wolf in lamb's clothing. The latex allergy in the sheepskin condom. It's all there, waiting for you to make some sort of sense out of it. To translate it so that others may translate and contextualize it. So that everyone has a shot at being an editor, at playing god with your mind.

When you were growing up in the mid-Georgia heat, swimming in the man-made lakes and sweating through the molasses-thick humidity, you remember you would hate getting dressed up every Sunday. The pleats in the front of your Bugle Boy khaki trousers rested so strangely against your too-thin thighs. The stiff starched cotton of the wrinkle-free button-up stuck to your skin, absorbing your perspiration and upping the temperature by twenty degrees. And when you stepped inside the Baptist Church, your father fussing with your hair, trying desperately to force the cowlick at your crown to stay down, you automatically held your breath.

Inside, the air-conditioned sanctuary would immediately freeze your sweat, dropping your temperature to an aching shiver. Even the pastor's compelling dissertation that you were certainly bound for the ever-lasting brimstone fires of Hell did nothing to warm your skin.

You. You would shiver and jostle your legs, squirming in the pew. You would wonder how it was that what the pastor said the Bible verse meant was so different from what your Sunday School teacher had said. Was so different from what your friends down at the Methodist Church had promised.

And you would wonder where it all came from. Your still-forming mind ripe with questions begging to be asked. To be answered. You would wonder how God got created. And who created the God that created the Adam. That created the Atom.

You would wonder who created religion in the first place. And where it lived for so long. And why it seemed so innate. And how people could be so trusting of it. How it could seem as innate as standing upright, as breathing, as avoiding fire.

You. You sit in your white room. The calm white. The erratic white. The white that your pastor used to describe Heaven. You search it for peace.

You write altruisms. You write aphorisms. You write religion.

You throw periods at the ends of sentences haphazardly. They branch off the curves of your handwriting. A quick flutter of a finger against the keyboard. Finalizing. Ending.

The Grace of the Lord Jesus be with God's people. Amen. Period.

Of the jinn and of mankind. Period.

An' it harm none...

And still this period seems so hard to place. Your hand refuses the dart-in-and-retreat necessary. It holds firm in its limenal space. In your threshold. Thresholds are where monsters live. Where you chose to become. Monster. Dead. Invisible. Awake. Alive. More.

Mark's.

You know that your words are finished. You have completed your task. What months have led you to. What Mark has led you to. You know that a dot, a simple smudge of ink against a page, does little to hold you in place, to hold your words stagnant. And maybe that's what you're afraid of. This twilight. Between the dog and the wolf.

Stagnancy would be much more welcomed.

Without thinking you feel your pen drop to the page. You feel your hands wrap around notebooks. Around loose papers covered in scribbled epitaphs, coffee stains. Drops of wax. Without thinking you feel your knees tense and straighten. You feel your lips purse together; you feel the breath push out from your lungs. You see the room go dark as candles extinguish.

Your manuscript is in your hands and all you want to do is sleep. All you can do is wonder why you blew out all the flames before you ignited the notebooks in your grasp, engulfed them in the hell you've been put through. All you want to do is dream away the world clutched in your hands.

Light pours in from the hallway as the door to your bedroom opens. Mark. Mark stands before you in a halo of fluorescent. He eyes you knowingly, his smirk almost a snarl to you now. You. Standing before your desk in what was utter darkness for — how long was it? You forget. Standing before your desk in silence, pupils expanding and contracting as the light around you adjusts. Wanes. Waxes.

The papers in your hands feel so heavy as you place them in Mark's. As you let go, relinquishing any hope of destruction. Or perhaps begetting hope. Or rather destruction.

Mark. Mark smiles. His teeth white in the darkness of your bedroom, the darkness engulfing his face.

Sleep.

You just wanted to be done. Now you are. You are finished.

Sleep.

Mark turns to the hallway. He places your papers in another set of hands. Mabel's? That foul-mouthed publisher's? Leonard's? You can't be sure. The light is too intense, is hurting your eyes.

Sleep.

Mark guides you to your bed. He removes your t-shirt and helps you sit. Helps your head find its pillow. Mark. He leans in to your cheek, lets his lips brush your eyelashes.

Butterfly kisses.

Mark. Mark's lips barely move as he whispers.

"It's not over yet."

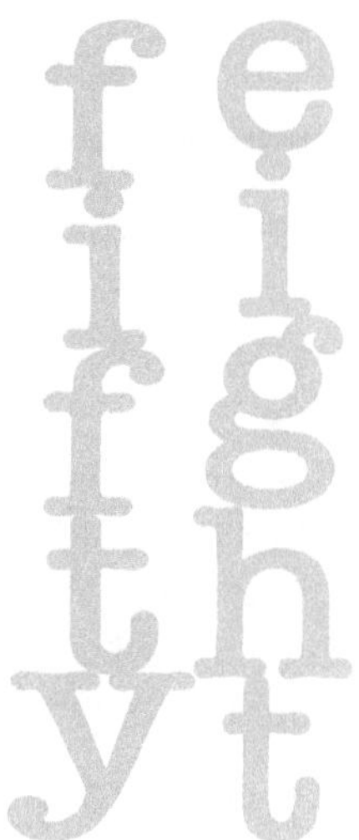

Your alarm clock sounds strange in its familiarity. Cracking and droning. It's been months since you heard its pulse, felt it's jarring force on your dreams, and still you find yourself humming along. Mentally denoting the time signature like it's a song you haven't heard in years but to which you can still remember the words.

You. You wonder if maybe this is a dream. You're having a hard time telling lately. You try to interpret the difference between years and minutes. Hours go by with you still singing the mechanical-cicada-chant meant to help you leave behind circadian rhythms. Cadences you never really let go of, no matter how loudly they buzz in your ear.

Minutes go by. You. You hit "snooze" every ten.

"Are you just going to let this go on forever?"

Mabel's skin glows in the blackness of your room. Mabel's porcelain white skin giving way to Lycra and jet-black hair. Her fingers stretch out along the wall, searching. A fluorescent bulb flickers on overhead. Adds to the hum of the alarm clock. Another sound you've not heard in what feels like centuries. The buzz.

"Get up. Mark's got food news. He's making breakfast."

You inhale the scent of frying pork fat. Of biscuits rising in the oven as your eyes adjust to the overhead light.

The living room stretches out before you, harsh and blinding. Echoes of time spent on the couch; of dream-fires and daggers turn somersaults in your optic nerves before fading into the banality of a room you never thought to fully study. The grey curtains pulled back beside the windows seem simultaneously paler and richer: bleached by the months of sunlight they absorbed for you, yet still such a powerful charcoal in relation to your white bedroom. The white of the page.

You could know this place in your dreams — you have known this place in your sleep — you were sleeping — right? And still your toe stubs against the metal army trunk pushed sideways against the couch; your arms flail up to stabilize your balance as your feet tie up in the area rug.

You. You stand in the doorway of the kitchen, feet spread shoulder length apart, unwilling to lean against the frame. Unwilling to allow yourself that sense of the casual.

Casualty.

So many casualties.

Mark. Mark has on his grey- and black-checked apron. His best Donna Reed smile.

"There's the star now," he says.

Mabel winks at you from the refrigerator door, pouring three glasses of orange juice and rolling her eyes to make you feel better about Mark's enthusiasm.

"Come on in!" Mark continues. "Don't play the stranger. This is your house too, after all."

You consider your words carefully, building up the bile resting in your lungs, desperate to enunciate the fatigue of captivity. Yet the words do not come.

"Oh, come on. It was for the best. Would you have finished the tome otherwise?" Mark. Mark could always read your mind. "Take a seat. I'm just finishing up the bacon, and I have really great news for you."

You sit pensively, waiting for the catch, eyes darting between Mark and Mabel, doing all they can to adjust.

"Why don't you have some breakfast and then you can go out and take a walk. Feel the wind in your hair and all of that. Just make sure you're back by seven." Mark smiles as he scoops scrambled eggs from the pan with a spatula and dumps them onto your plate. He catches your eyes with his smile. "It's not a curfew. You're free to go. Just, you know, be back by seven. I have a surprise. For you. Eat up."

fifty nine

The sun, when it angles around the grey-soaked clouds, feels shallow on your skin, barely brushing your cheek. You wonder if its the feeling of newness you're experiencing — how the leaves seem to be so green they're vibrating, how the sidewalk seems so firm, seems to be moving so quickly beneath your feet — that's creating this disembodied notion of self. You, whatever you you are outside of your physical being, rest a few inches above and behind your eyes. You hold up your hands, clench your fingers tight against your palms, watch your knuckles go white, and wait for a tingling sensitivity that never comes. You tell your fingers to relax and drop your arms to dangle at your sides.

The sky, despite being overcast, seems alive, glowing. Each car that barrels past moves slower than it should, at least you think it's moving slowly, giving you time to memorize every plastic line in every grill, to read all the bumper stickers, to admire the vibrant paint jobs named after fruits that would never reach that color naturally. Only at the corners of your eyes, resting in the margins of your peripheral vision, does the world before you retain the gritty, smog-filled haze you're used to seeing. But you can't look at it directly. It's as shifty as you're feeling.

You only see what you're wanting to see.

You. You think that laughing could help you reach catharsis. Could you help you realize your accomplishment. The ending. The tome. You think that it should be that sudden, rumbling kind of laughter; the kind riddled with giddiness like the why-didn't-I-see-it-before movie moments for the hero. For the mad scientist. You. You think that laughter, that your laughing alone in the street would only mark a glimmer of insanity. Would give all those passing people whom you think are looking at you a reason to actually stare.

"Have you accepted Jesus Christ as your Lord and Savior?"

"What?" You stare at the kid who's stepped before you on the sidewalk, stopping to size you up as you return the favor. His curly red hair is cropped short, bleached to a near blond by a summer spent on the streets as a local missionary. His thin lips are more orange than pink, matching the thick freckles that splatter across the bridge of his nose, across his pale cheeks.

This kid, he stares at you with his green eyes, eyes that glint and sharpen with the contrasting orange stripes on his tie. This kid, he stares at you and says, "You look like someone who's lost his way."

You wonder if "his" was meant to be capitalized, if the boy in front of you is looking to show you God's way. You want to tell him it's too late. You want to speak, but your voice rests like an atrophied muscle in your larynx.

The boy's face falls slightly. His eyes scrunch and his face settles into his age, into his youth. For the first time you notice the tell-tell sign of a young lifer, a metal ring in his right eyebrow. He eyes you suspiciously, noticing that you are freshly showered, that your clothes are nice, or at least not standard psych-ward issue. You. You find him fascinating.

While he sizes you up again, you watch the spark enter his eye, telling him that he's found his mark, his target. His way into the eternal glory of sainthood. The wayward soul he can save.

You finally find your voice.

"Sorry, man. I'm not really interested in what you're selling." You begin to walk away, checking your watch and turning back in the direction of your house. Mark's house.

"Are you lost?"

"I, uh— I know my way home."

You listen to his footsteps drawing closer behind you but do nothing to slow your pace. Or to quicken it.

"But do you know your way to His home? To the eternal home that could be yours?" He catches up and steps in front of you. You consider sidestepping him, but decide to stop. "Are you lost?" he repeats.

You repeat things so you can remember them. For their Pavlovian rewards. This kid, he repeats things with altered inflection, hoping he won't have to delve deeper, to enter into a philosophy he's not too sure he fully understands. He repeats things to test the theory of chance. Four "no"s for every "yes."

"I've really got to get back to my house."

You wonder if lying to a self-proclaimed missionary is akin to coveting your mother and father or murdering your neighbor's ass. You have over an hour before your curfew. The curfew Mark swears is not a curfew. Mark. Mark tells you you're free. And still your feet angle toward your door, toward your whitewashed bedroom.

"Are you looking for an escape from the prison of our modern world? From the sin and temptation that plague our souls and our hearts?"

His speech would probably be a lot more effective if his voice wasn't still cracking while his vocal chords stretch and settle into their adult positions. Still, you feel the city closing in around you. The air grows tight, then stale, then dissipates. All around you the concrete looms, the asphalt covers the soil. You wait for the trees, the birds, the goddamn flowerbeds to do something. Nature abhors a vacuum. You're sure you learned that in a high school science class, that Aristotle held that theory before Pan had died and Christ was born. And that's what this is. This is what you're feeling. A vacuum. But the pigeons won't do a goddamn thing.

And again, *feral* is a misuse of the word.

You feel yourself surrounded by white. The blinds shut. Tight. You. You're examining the deadbolt, gleaming silver steel in the thin crack between the door and the frame. You try to will it to move, but know it's useless. Hopeless. The opposite of the survival instinct. The opposite of feral. The cold complacency. The lay-down-and-die.

"Why don't you come with me?"

The red-headed boy extends his hand. He can see the fortitude stripped from your expression. He indicates a car in the lot down the street with his slender fingers, his freckled hand. You nod and head that way, keeping your eyes down so he won't see them darting, won't see them betraying the thought processes burrowing through your mind.

You. You're taking a mental inventory of everything in your room. You're wondering if there's anything you can't live without. You're thinking you'll get to whatever church or halfway house this kid's got in mind and call your parents and ask them to send you some money. Then you can slip back to your street late at night to get your car. Maybe you'll go by The Morning Bean and beg for your job back. Or better yet, maybe you should move out of state. Or out of the country.

"— You do look a little skinny. And you're awfully pale."

Suddenly you realize the boy is talking to you. His knuckles are white against the steering wheel and he's keeping his eyes trained straight ahead with the wide rigidity of someone afraid to look away from the street for even a second. Of someone who just got their license and is driving his father's car.

"What are they like?" he continues.

"What are what like?"

"Drugs. I've never tried any. I mean I *wouldn't* try any if I had the opportunity. It's just not God's way, you know. But. What are they like?"

This boy's convinced himself that you must be a druggie. Some rich kid user who's just wandering the streets looking for his next score. You don't bother to tell him that his pastor's kids are probably a better bet for that than you.

"I don't do drugs," you say, conceding on your thoughts and turning your attention to the kid. "I've just had a lot on my mind lately."

"Is it alcohol then?"

"Why do you assume that because I don't have the light of your Christ in my eye I must be compulsively on some mind-altering substance? If you ask me, reading the Bible will give you a hell of a lot more reasons to drink than reasons to exclaim some cathartic song of joy."

The kid purses his lips for a moment, and you suppress a smile as you watch one spread across his lips. Not only has he convinced himself he's bringing in a druggie, he's got a Satanist on his hands to boot. You watch his face drop. Either he's checking himself for his pride or.... Yep. You watch as he inches slowly towards the driver's side door in his seat, trying to look casual as he puts distance between the two of you.

He pulls the car into the parking lot of an old public elementary school. He parks in the roundabout used by the school buses and the two of you head toward the open doors of what is most likely the cafeteria.

"We do a soup kitchen here twice a month. I'm sure there's someone here you can talk to. Someone who can help you get back on your feet."

You roll your eyes and keep a lookout for a payphone, figuring you'll probably be out of luck since little kids rarely have a need to call the track to play the horses.

You step from the asphalt to the sidewalk and make for the doors just as a blond woman exits, digging through her purse for her car keys. She looks up and stops short.

"What are you doing here?" Jude asks. "Shouldn't you be at home, getting ready for your party?"

You look at her questioningly.

"Oh. Ooops," she blushes. "Surprise."

Jude looks to the boy at your side and a smile spreads slowly across her face.

"Trevor," she says and the boy stands at attention. "Not every city dweller you meet is a druggie-Satanist."

Trevor drops his head and kicks at the cement with his heel. You sort of feel sorry for the kid.

"I may very well be an alcoholic though."

Trevor's face brightens and Jude smirks, shaking her head slightly from side to side.

"Why don't you go inside, Trevor. See if they need any help cleaning up. Your dad's around somewhere. I'm sure he'll want to know his car is back in one piece."

Trevor nods and heads toward the door, looking back at you as you shrug and silently thank him for attempting to Harriet Tubman you to freedom.

"I'll give you a ride back to your house," Jude offers. "Please don't tell Mark I spoiled the surprise."

Mark put balloons on the mailbox. Red, black, white, and helium-filled, shifting in the late evening breeze. Jude slips her car adeptly down the narrow street before parallel parking it in the closest space to your house.

You step out of the vehicle and onto what's left of the sidewalk after years of city neglect let the concrete crack to make way for crabgrass and dandelions. Jude circles around the car and joins your walk toward the door.

"I'm really excited about your work," Jude says, stopping her pace just below the porch steps. "It really is amazing that you finished so quickly."

"Have you read what I wrote?" you ask incredulously. "You shouldn't get too excited about it."

"Oh, you're just being modest," Jude assures you. "It's not often one can produce such a prophetic tome. You should be proud."

The door opens and Mark steps out to the porch, eyes bright, smiling. He nods to Jude and steps forward to put his arm around your shoulders.

"You really should be proud," he says, leading you in doors. "We all are."

Your living room is a flurry of motion. Alia and Haripreet, Ambyrr and Matthew, Mabel, Clara, Justin and Leonard and Betty Ann. They are all spread about the room, chatting, laughing, reveling. The setting sun pouring through the curtained windows casts a red haze over everything, creating a strange tint on your guests' skin. They seem demonic in the light; you can almost see horns and tails, storybook style, before you blink at Mark's grasp on your arm and you settle back into reality.

Mark leads you the few steps toward the center of the room and raises your arm triumphantly into the air, like the boxer who's just managed to keep his head off the matt a few seconds longer than his opponent.

"Everyone," Mark calls. "The guest of honor has arrived! And congratulations are in order. Malcolm Young has agreed to not only represent the work, but has already found a publisher ready to pick it up for distribution!"

The room applauds and you blush. You. You're trying to figure out what these people think you wrote. These people who thought you were interviewing them for college papers, for conversion, for fun. You're wondering if Mark just told them the paper had evolved, that the desire to become translated into the desire to convert. You're wondering if each of these people is so sure in their faith that they feel you could not have placed their own spirituality at risk within your tome. You're trying to remember what you wrote in the first place, if you wrote at all. You're trying to figure out why your guests suddenly have halos, why you can suddenly see their bones.

You shake the hallucination from your eyes as you take a seat on the couch, accepting the beer from Mabel and congratulatory comments from the line forming to shake your hand.

"You know, boy," Leonard guffaws as he shakes your hand with his left one, not wanting to shake off Betty Ann who's latched onto his right elbow, "I didn't figure you'd have it in you. But I guess if Mark saw something in you, I shoulda known."

Betty Ann releases her grasp on her husband's arm and leans forward, hugging you awkwardly.

"Don't worry," she whispers into your ear, "I won't tell Lenny what exactly it was that Mark saw in you. Or put in you."

She retreats back to Leonard's elbow, smiling pure sugarcane as her eyes gleam in the space between anger and amusement. Leonard smiles and gives you one more "you did good, kid" before making his way toward the kitchen for another beer.

Ambyrr's Earth-Mother shrug hangs loosely from her shoulders; her frizzy brown hair seems more teased out than usual, more electric. It brushes your face as she sits to your right, the bounce of the cushions from her plop down countered to a faint ripple by the wave of Justin's plunk to your left. Justin leans back, wrapping his arm around you. You feel him squeeze your shoulder tightly, pulling you toward him with the strained enthusiasm of someone who has not been allowed much human contact in the past year.

The Wiccan and the Olosha go about with their joyous, sycophantic words, both jockeying for attention and smiling from ear to ear. For a moment, you wonder the extent of Justin's excitement, before you start to realize, before you just know that the hard object pressing into your thigh is a sheathed ceremonial knife clipped to his belt. As you sense Ambyrr's athame tucked away beneath her long shrug, you force the obligatory smile across your lips and excuse yourself to the kitchen for another beer.

As you stand, you think for a moment that you can see the bones beneath their skin. You shake the vision from your eyes.

As you stand, you hear a loud pop and fight the urge to hit the deck. Mabel smiles proudly as the bottle of champagne in her hands bubbles over slightly to the carpeting before she catches it in plastic flutes and begins passing them around the room. Her porcelain white skin seems whiter against the imagined wings you see on her back. The wings disappear to be replaced by bones. To be replaced by Mabel.

It's as if you're seeing the entire room through a pair of those X-Ray specs you'd get from a Cracker Jack box, from the back page of a ten-cent comic.

As Mabel continues to pass around the bubbly, you set your step toward the front door.

"Hey, hey," Mark says, cutting you off as you reach for the knob. "This toast is for you."

"I really don't get what we're celebrating," you insist. "I just need a cigarette."

Outside the sun has set completely and the invasive dusk brings with it an eerie silence that seems completely incongruous with the party behind you. Like in front of you, waiting for you to step off of the porch is Limbo. Like behind you, waiting for you to step off the porch is Heaven or Hell or Nirvana or Utopia or the Abyss or Hades. As if either way holds eternal damnation.

Your cigarette tastes odd and you watch the cherry glow orange down the end of your nose, allowing it to fill your vision, to blur at the edges. To consume you.

"Do you mind if I get a hit?"

You turn toward Mark, offering your smoke, not surprised when your optic nerve flashes from a skeletal shell to Mark's stubbled jaw and smirking smile.

"I think this whole progression really fucked me up," you say, not bothering to place the blame for Mark's seclusionary part in the process. Figuring that to be understood.

Mark. Mark simply smiles.

"You've been through a lot," he says. "Allowing yourself to open up like that. To pour out. That's no small feat. That's why we're celebrating.

"You took something beautiful out of yourself. You placed it out there for the world."

"Like Adam's rib?" you ask, sarcastically.

"Better," Mark smiles. "Better because this is something you gave of your own volition. Not something some sculptor with a god-complex stole to make himself a fuck buddy."

Your single expression of humor lies somewhere between a snort and a sigh. You look at Mark. His eyes are glowing against the night sky, reflecting the streetlamps shining through the oak and magnolia tree leaves lining your street.

"I missed you," you finally say. "I mean, I missed people in general. But I really missed you. I should be pissed as mother fucking hell at you, but all I can think is how much I really did miss seeing that goddamn smirk on your face."

This was not what you expected to be saying. This is not the catharsis you were expecting.

You throw in a quick "asshole" just for good measure and smile in your roommate's direction. Relishing your moments together. Alone.

Mark bites his bottom lip, leaning against the railing of the porch, straightening his arms and lifting his body up onto his toes. He lets his heels fall to the ground and looks at you as if he's had his own grand realization. Finally, he turns to you. He turns to you and he says:

"I miss you too."

Five years ago, you heard this in the past tense. Five years ago you heard two extra letters. Five years later you notice the nuance. You can pick up on the foreshadowing.

But tonight. Tonight you are trying to smile as you put out your cigarette. Tonight you are trying to train your eyes to stop jack-knifing between visions of heaven and hell, to stop showing your friends and houseguests as skeletons with horns, as corpses with wings. Tonight you are mostly wondering if Mark is going to kiss you.

And he does. Quickly. Gently. A single peck on your lips before turning to the door.

"We should get back inside," he says, nodding his head softly as if to affirm himself of the correct course of action. "The party is just beginning."

Your mood deepens as you step back into the living room. You feel the slight tinge of insanity, the hint of terror return. Perched around the room, flanking each wall, forming a circle, your party guests stand with their champagne.

You feel your head spinning.

But it is not something you are a part of. You are detached, removed from your body. As you reel, your eyes dance from person to person. Lighting on Mabel and her jet-black hair. Slinking over Ambyrr and Justin. Across Haripreet's smile; Alia's demure wink. You catch on Leonard's bright-eyed smile and Betty Ann's shrugging glare. You feel the sneer in Clara's eyes down to your core. You sense the wonder within Jude and Matthew. And the solemnity buried behind Mark's jovial announcement.

"Here's the man of the hour, folks," he smiles, and flutes rise in a toast while Mabel places a glass of the carbonated liquid into your grasp.

You quickly take a sip and let your hand fall to your side, trying to force out a smile as your eyes again begin to flash toward the demonic. Toward the angelic.

You. You feel yourself crash back into your body. Feel your skin pulsing, your heart pounding, your head throbbing. You cast your eyes down at the champagne in your cup, fighting the urge to wobble with the rhythm of your palpitating frame.

When you again peer up, the circle seems to have moved closer, tightening around you. You see concern spread across Mark's face. You see a leering excitement spread across the others, as if they are wolves on the scent of a wounded fawn, drug dogs jonesing for the kilo of cocaine condomed inside the mule's ass or the bimbo's silicon implants.

"Are you feeling alright?" Mabel asks, stepping closer to put her hand on your forehead.

Quickly you pull away from her reach, feeling your back come in swift contact with the door.

As they step closer, you flash between visions of gargoyles and Greek statues. You see knives. Not the pretty ones, not the jeweled and delicate blades that act as focal points on altars or in ceremony. Not the dull gold-hilted knives, but the dirty and sharp ones. The ones used when the pomp is left behind and the actual ritual begins. The ones that don't need to be visually pleasing to the gods because their eyes are glazed over and bloodthirsty.

The ones that are begging for a sacrifice.

You. You feel like you are re-living a dream. You are waiting for Mark to ask you to become a martyr. For the cause. To boost your book sales. To get the message out.

You try to push yourself through the closed door, attempting to back through the unyielding wood as the crowd around you closes in. Their eyes seem hollow. Their jaws twist and their bared teeth snake into macabre smiles.

You drop your champagne to the floor and reach frantically for the doorknob, trying to turn it, trying to maneuver enough room to slip from the house. To make a run for it.

You. You feel your lungs grow tight. You brace yourself for the first swipe of metal across your skin. For the feel of the cold steel, for the sharpness that stings first. The sharpness that saves the ache for later.

And suddenly, everything is black.

You awake sabruptly, your alertness almost fooling you to believe you are still dreaming. The ceiling above you is familiar, though it seems more distant, physically, from you and not as white as you remember it being, water stains producing yellowed designs and cracking the paint. Your bed, too, holds a sort of familiar dissonance. It does not seem as comfortable as it had, or as large.

Your eyes adjust to the afternoon sunlight seeping into the windows as you pull your torso up to a seated position and let your feet find the floor. The blinds are gone. Your door is gone, ripped right off its hinges. Or rather unscrewed and removed. There's a definite delicacy to it, a softness and an electric screwdriver. Either way, though, it is gone.

You stand quickly and angle your feet toward the doorway, allowing your hand to shuffle through the papers scattered over your desk. You recognize your handwriting. You see its strain across sentences and ideas.

Across the hallway, the door to Mabel's room stands open, showcasing the openness, the lack of powdered wigs or bookcases lining the soft purple walls. You know it's pointless to check further and instead turn to your right and through the bathroom door. You pull your toothbrush from the medicine cabinet and reach for the tap. Nothing. No water. Nothing from the shower. Even the shallow pool in the well of the toilet has the soft tan ring of a hard water stain, the glistening glaze of stagnancy.

"This is really not funny, guys," you call out, tossing your toothbrush into the sink and turning toward the door. You let your eyes find the small black drops of hair dye still staining the tiles from when Mark died your hair.

You cross into the living room, unsurprised to find it cleared out as well. The smoke from fires built before the flue was opened clings to the dark brick façade surrounding the pit. The removed area rug reveals a dark hardwood floor, still scuffed from the legs of chairs and couches despite the protection of the dark grey carpet. The only thing left is the army chest, its latch unhooked, waiting in almost the center of the room.

You're expecting Mark to jump out with a "Surprise!" of a "Gotcha!" or an "April Fools!" or a "We sunk everything into your book and it bombed!" as you approach the chest. You feel your left cheek twist upward, doing your best to mimic the sarcastic glare of Mark's smirk with your own. Your foot meets the chest hard, trying to get the one-up on Mark first. Instead, the chest tips over easily, the lid falling back and allowing an old pencil and a marble to roll out, pool-ball to the corner, and stop abruptly on the heating vent grate.

"I give you props on being thorough," you yell toward the ceiling, toward Mark's room, listening to a shuffle and thump.

You rush through the kitchen, empty as well as far as you can tell, to the stairway leading up. You bound over the ragged brown carpeting and fling open the door at the top. Everything is how you remembered it; all the bookshelves lining the walls are still covered with volumes of leather-bound books, seeming endless in their range and age.

At the foot of his bed, atop the army green chest nearly identical to the one downstairs, sits a twelve-inch screen with a VCR. And Mabel's videocassettes. No note. No Mark.

You pull over the rolling chair from Mark's desk, surprised to see a bound volume of your own text sitting there. You take it into your hands and flip through the pages tentatively. Your free hand reaches for the first tape in Mabel's series. You slip it into the VCR and push your gaze to the screen as it shifts from blue to a test panel to Mabel, younger, too close to the camera, adjusting the focus from the wrong side before taking a few steps back, a few deep breaths.

"I met a guy today," she finally says, and her eyes light up with the naiveté that comes with the crossbreed of intellectual and sexual stimulation. The naiveté you remember from yourself. "He's got the greyest eyes and the cutest fucking smile."

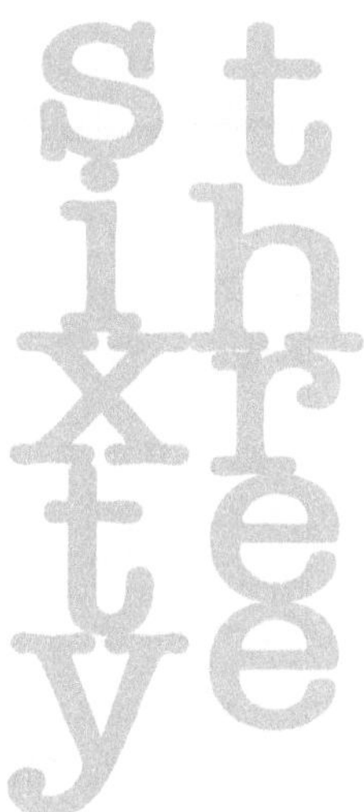

You. You shouldn't be surprised by the videotapes. You shouldn't be surprised to see Mabel. To see Mark. To hear Mabel question Haripreet and Justin and Alia. To watch Ambyrr giggle and chitter away for hours. Until the tape runs out. You should have expected to see Matthew and Clara and Jude. To hear Leonard's bellowing guffaw.

You.

You should have seen the planning behind Mark's eyes all along, resting there behind his smirk, behind his laughter. Behind his sex. But there's really no way you could have known.

The story is inside of you already.

You only see what you're wanting to see.

There's no way you could have known.

You repeat things so you can remember them. The details. The tidbits of your life, of the life going on around you that the shrink would want to know. That the police would want to know. That Mark would know.

Mark, omnipotent being that he is, asking you about lie detectors and philosophy. Spirituality.

You. You have never been one to look for the god particle. To find Jesus in your mashed potatoes or the Virgin Mary hanging out in your stool. To look for Zeus in bestiality porn. Or Buddha in the fat guy at the bus stop.

You tune yourself to the details of the faces that pass over the TV screen, some of them younger, some seem older, but they are all definitely the people you interviewed — the folks you saw cascading between the horrendous and the glorious, closing in on you with knives.

Their expressions jump with each stop and start of the camera, with each cut Mabel decided upon. The phrases she chose to leave out. The words you choose to omit.

The truth that lies there. The falsity.

You listen to the stories, recognizing the familiar cadence of the words spoken into the sagging boom mic that dips into frame at odd intervals. You hear Ambyrr chat away about her fairy tattoo, Haripreet reach his enlightened epiphanies. Leonard's stories of executions and dime store drama captured on videotape.

You are surprised that Clara looks roughly fifteen years older than when you first walked into her office. You wonder at Alia's ability to look the exact same age. How Jude managed to shave a decade from her life while Matthew appears to have put on at least two.

You know the story is in the pieces you're missing; that it lies somewhere in the frames that were clipped out. Eighteen videocassettes and you have no idea what the hell's been going on other than that Mark is truly a master of the elaborate set-up.

You wait for a two-bit television actor to pop out with his camera and a bevy of laugh-track laughter.

You swallow hard.

As you reach to turn off the television, you notice another tape at the foot of Mark's bed, barely poking out from beneath the red and black quilt folded across the mattress. A "nineteen" is scrawled lightly in pencil across the sticker. It matches Mabel's handwriting, but obviously it wasn't placed here by her. No, this has Mark written all over it.

The videocassette feels warm against your palm, and you cup your hands around it until they tingle. You know that this is the edit. The core. The words better left unsaid. The words dying to be placed into the open.

As you load the mini DV tape into the player, you see the faces of those who've become your instructors, your taunters.

Your teacher. Your lover.

"I was born in—"

"I am two thousand and twelve years old—"

"I began my life in—"

"How does one quantify a lifetime?"

"I'm seventeen, right? Or three. Or three millennia. But for all intents and purposes, I'm seventeen. Isn't that how this works? Seventeen by the mortal model. But as far as reinventions go, I've lost count."

You hear a snicker from off-camera, then Mabel's voice, clipping from its proximity to the built-in microphone.

"Mark, come on," she giggles. "You're supposed to be taking this seriously. How am I going to create this masterpiece film you say I'm destined to create if you're making up this bullshit?"

Mark's smirk leaks across the screen, taunting, hypnotic. He stares directly at the lens of the camera, as if he's looking through it. As if he's leering straight through the years and digital image capturing to peer directly into your eyes. He opens his mouth slowly, breathing gently as he says, "You can decide what's serious when you're done editing the footage. Then just leave it in a pile on the cutting room floor." His eyes move up, out of the frame, no doubt locking on Mabel's, taking in her porcelain skin and teenage goth rebellion. "But while you're snipping away, consider your obsession with headpieces of the sixteenth century." His eyes direct back to the lens, again locking on yours. "Think about your obsession with the immortality of words."

You feel a shiver rush down your spine, sobering you, suddenly bringing your champagne-induced headache into focus. You squint your eyes from the pain. You revisit the visions of the night before.

"You aren't who you think you are."

Mark seems so confident in his words. So confident he seems ready for the asylum.

"Really?" Mabel asks incredulously. "Who do I think I am? And besides which, who the hell is ever who they say they are?"

There is amusement in Mark's eyes. His face remains still in the frame. He seems so calm, so unbothered. So much less agitated than the Mark who would exuberate the pains of the mortal flesh, of childbirth, of law, of life. He almost seems... serene.

"I suppose no one is who they say they are," he finally says. "But you, Mabel Atrickson, are not the young girl from Lilburn who liked playing with GI Joes more than Barbies. You are not merely the young woman who preferred *The Story of O* to *Pride and Prejudice*."

Mabel grows silent behind the camera. You can imagine the confusion on her face as deeply as you can feel your own.

Mark's voice is gentle in its even cadence. He speaks matter-of-factly and channels all of his charm through his eyes.

"We all have a role to play," he says. He says, "You would be surprised what you can discover about yourself."

He says things about "both sides" and "all sides" and "minutiae" and "grandness." He mentions challenges and outcomes. He mentions the mortal soul versus the immortal entity: the god-form.

"So, you're God?" you ask aloud, in unison with Mabel's skeptical voice emitting from the television speakers.

Well, this explains a good deal of Mark's manipulation. Of his self-righteous attitude. Delusions of grandeur are tricky things.

But the smile on Mark's face is genuine. Glowing, even.

"Not in the least," he says. "That would assume that one could be god. That god could be.

"No, right now, I am simply Mark. Still I am doubt, and I am temptation. Just as you, Mabel, are temptation—"

You can feel Mabel's cheeks grow bright red, her libido liven, even through the years, even though she is off-screen, there it is, still captured on tape.

"—are retorts and questioning. Just as Harry is wonder, and Justin is discovery. Just as Matthew is understanding, and Jude is care. You are a part of this, you play as large a part as Clara's rigidity, or Ambyrr's inclusion, or Alia's push forward."

Mark's face is still not giving up the joke. He's sitting firm, wrapped up in his thoughts. He's trying to press this as far as it will go. You roll your eyes and reach toward the monitor to turn it off, missing Mark, but glad you escaped whatever cult he'd ushered Mabel into relatively unscathed.

As your finger lands on the power button, Mark's voice catches your attention.

"In five years time," he says. Mark says, "In five years time, we will meet a writer...."

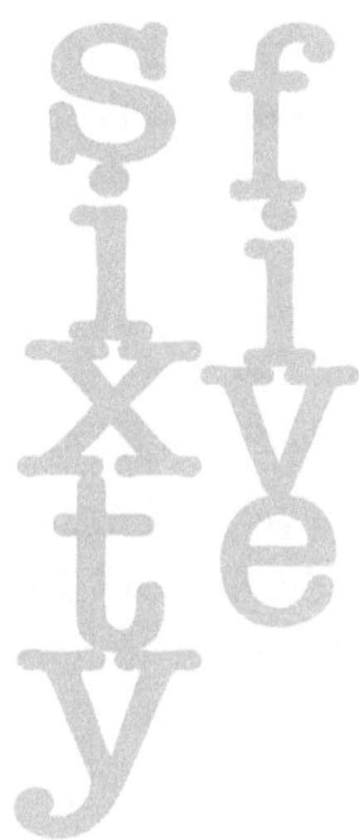

It's five years later and you're sitting on the patio of an independent coffee shop on the verge of selling out to a franchisee, sipping your iced latte and flipping through your notebooks. You're listening to the sounds of the evening roll past your eardrums. Meditating on the click of the pen, the scratch of the tip on the paper, the deposit of ink left behind.

At your apartment, all of Mark's books line the walls. You. You packed them up and took them with you. You figured they were left for you. You packed them up and moved out of the city, off to the small university town northeast from your mythical coming-of-age.

Sometimes you go back to the city, drive down the small narrow street, and stare at the empty lot where your house once stood. The neighbors tell you it has been vacant for years, that it was crumbling at the edges for years before that. They tell you a few months back a tree limb swung free in a storm and tore through the roof. That after that, when the homeless and vagabonds would try to spend the night indoors they would get their feet stuck when the floorboards gave way and need stitches or run off screaming barely lucid rantings about visions of skeletons with wings, of demons and of gods. They tell you that the city eventually just bulldozed the place to keep the riff-raff out and the neighbors happy.

You've read through most of Mark's tomes. Your own, the bound copy of the work you'd written, is placed on the bottom shelf of the final case. To be the culmination. To allow you to revisit. To reacquaint yourself with your death.

You've read stories of the jokes the Greek Gods would play on the mortals, the tests and trials they would put the humans through. The revelry the Gods would garner.

You've read descriptions of the monotheistic roots to all religions, of that single god who popped out all the representations, of how the mortal mind was too weak to identify the whole and named all the parts.

You've read of the singing and the dancing and the possession and the force of the holy.

You've identified the saints and their victories, the martyrs and their selflessness, the angels and the demons and their components.

You read about the Archangel Michel and the demon Mephistopheles, sitting together and betting on humanity. Heads or tails on the fate of the mortal city. You read about them picking out a man to test, to determine the outcome.

And here you are, God's whipping boy.

Sometimes you think you see Mark. He's walking in the opposite direction on the sidewalk on the opposite side of the street. He's driving through the fast food drive thru while you're going inside. He's crawling into bed with you at night, or he's smirking his smirk from behind the windshield of a passing car.

Temptation.

The numbers you had for Mark's friends, Mark's family are disconnected. Ambyrr's house is empty save for the unmistakable odor of cats. Haripreet's apartment is bare. Clara's dental office is a pediatrics center.

Sometimes. Sometimes you question your sanity. You ask your family about those months and they say they never met Mark but that you spoke very highly of him. Sometimes you question your ability to remember.

Five years pass and you learn to breathe differently, to view the world in a different light, through squinted eyes and a sneering smirk.

Not that you're angry.

On the contrary, you are amused.

You pick up your book, your sweat, your words. You turn it over in your hands and study the binding, rub your fingers along the blue-black cloth covering the hard casing.

You close your eyes briefly, sighing deeply as you pull back the cover, ready at last to revisit those months of longing, of solitude.

You are surprised to see Mark's handwriting dripping across the page. You. You are surprised to see today's date right down to the year, the address to a coffee shop in your new town. The address to the coffee shop you spend your nights at, fighting hard to regain the focus the expulsion of words to paper takes.

You close your eyes as you close the book cover, reveling in the idea that Mark could be at your destination but knowing that won't be the case.

Temptation. Doubt.

It's five years later and you're buckling the seatbelt in your car, steering toward the street, toward the bicycle-spoke-windmill, toward the test.

Mark. Mark is gone. His smirking smile, his gentle confidence.

But you are here. Smirking. Smiling. Humming a little hymn.

He only hears what he's wanting to hear.

The low bass of a muffler on Gaines School. The clasp of a car door closing. The rumble and whine of the engine in a truck the pizza delivery guy just got into.

He only hears what he's wanting to hear.

The soft click, click of the bicycle spokes some local artist turned into a windmill and cemented outside of the coffee shop. All the noise pollution of an early summer night in the south.

He, himself, is hunched over a notebook on a cement patio table. He, omnipotent being that he is, knows every song on every radio of every car that passes. He can hear the conversation the Sorority Girls inside are having between placing their drink orders.

www.ingramcontent.com/pod-product-compliance
Lightning Source LLC
Chambersburg PA
CBHW030817310726
48980CB00006B/523/J

* 9 7 8 0 5 7 8 0 2 9 5 1 1 *